Tequila, slammed

Deborah Carter

Facebook;	@debbiecarter27
Twitter;	@CDeborah6
Instagram;	@debbiecarter27
Website;	www.deborahcarterauthor.com
Email;	authordeborahcarter@gmail.com

Also, by this Author

Addison

Gripping the railing, sticky with salt spray and God only knows what else, I leant as far over as possible while still maintaining a safe footing and watched as my stomach contents disappear below roiling and froth tipped waves. My muscles clenched on my achingly hollow stomach as though attempting to squeeze every last dreg from me. The dry urging began in earnest as the rolling swell of the ship undulated beneath me. It was probably a mistake coming up on deck, but I'd hoped the fresh air would help with the raging seasickness. I raised my head, my sallow-skinned face tilted skyward toward the seething mass of dark, rain-filled clouds and screamed my frustration from a bile blistered throat at having to return to the god-forsaken Island.

Tears rained from sleep-deprived, reddened eyes and mingled with the pelting droplets plummeting from the heavens above, almost as if they cried right along with me. How had my life fallen apart so completely? Nate's summons coming out of the blue had been a shock all its own, but to see him, skin and bone, so desperately ill on his death bed when I arrived at the hospital, had thrown me. I had so not expected to hear from him and especially under these circumstances.

His face wan, breathing laboured and his whispered words a riddle. "Addison, you have to remember!" he pulled the oxygen mask aside; his eyes, glazed from the pain medication, fought to focus on me. "He wasn't mine." He rasped. "Rhett isn't my..." he dropped the mask, the elastic pinging it back into place as his head slid sideways and his eyes stared as the machine went ballistic, screaming along with me.

Garrett

Standing behind a rust-reddened girder, I was transfixed, watching the woman clinging precariously to the ship's railing. Was she going to climb up and fling herself overboard? And if she was, could I reach her in time to prevent her plummet of doom? No, I conceded to myself, not COULD I, but WOULD I?

She looked so different from the teenage girl I remembered. Gone were the blonde streaks with the blue-lagoon tips from her vibrant red halo of hair; those eerily dark shadowed eyes and sharp cheekbones, lean body, almost too skinny and her long, long legs that seemed to go on forever.

Now, as I scrutinised her curvaceous figure as she leant over the side, I noted that she'd filled out in all the right places; hips and arse lusciously rounded; perfectly plump pillows in which to rest one's cock between on cold nights. *Where the hell had that thought come from? She didn't belong to me anymore; I couldn't be thinking that way about her.* And yet, as Addie threw back her head to scream at the sky, my eyes devoured the upward thrust of those beautiful breasts, and my cock twitched.

Her screams brought it all back; three long, lonely years melted away, transporting me back in time to when those earth-shattering screams were my fault.

My hand gingerly supported her back as I attempted to assist her down the steps to the waiting ambulance when I was caught off-guard by a vicious jab to my ribcage from her bony elbow, and my breath left my lungs in a rush of air. "Don't touch me," she snarled and ripped herself away from my hands, and I could do nothing but watch as those dark eyes glared at me as she backed away. When she lost her footing, my hands reached out to capture her windmilling arms, but to no avail, she fell, toppling over and over down to the cold hard ground below. She lay motionless and broken, head and shoulders on the gravelled driveway and her feet, legs and her nearly full-term pregnant belly balancing precariously on the two lower steps. I saw her stomach contract, an internal kick, vicious enough to be seen from where I'd frozen in place at the top of the stone staircase, and then all was still.

Paramedics were fast, but I was faster as I came to my senses and seemingly flew down to where Addie, my darling nymph, had fallen. "Addie," I whispered as I held her head in one hand and brushed the blue tips of hair away from her closed eyes with the other. "Addie, can you hear me?"

As the paramedic knelt, I released her, my hand coming away red, sticky from the blood oozing from an unseen wound, and then I noticed the large red mass colouring the stones beneath her hips. I knew. I knew the baby was gone. Kneeling silently beside her as guilt and grief crept up. I knew beyond doubt that she'd never forgive me for this; hell, I would never forgive myself. I held her hand as the ambulance crew checked for her pulse. "She's alive," one said, and I heard nothing else, allowing those two words to play repeatedly in my head as I shuffled back to enable them to do their jobs. The paramedics supported Addie's head, carefully manoeuvring her body onto the stretcher, strapped down and lifted into the back of the decrepit old vehicle. My last sight of her pale, blood-streaked face would haunt me as she was driven away amidst a spray of gravel and a screaming siren, the sound becoming inaudible as the ambulance turned away, and I was alone, still on my knees in the empty silence. Raising my face to the darkening sky, I did something I'd never done in my entire life. I prayed, prayed she would survive and that she would one day forgive me!

Now Addie was screaming again, only this time it wasn't at me. Three years of cruel silence had me almost believing I no longer cared, and now, listening to the high-pitched keening coming from her lips, I knew I was lying to myself, as the sound shredded what she'd left of my broken heart.

Addison

The ship continued to kick like a bronco on rodeo day; my stomach, now achingly empty, continued to spasm uncomfortably, and the buffeting wind and lashing rain plastered the black, heavy material of my mourning dress to my body. The cold finally began to penetrate, and I knew I'd have to abandon my post on deck and succumb to the lonely, claustrophobic cabin below. I hated sailing this route. A journey I'd experienced a few times in my youth had me securing one of the few cabins; it was by far the easiest and most convenient way to cross the choppy channel. I preferred a little privacy instead of trying to sleep in the chair rows on the upper deck. I'd vowed never to set foot again on this old bucket of nuts and bolts, but not because of the brutal seasickness; no, I was genuinely fearful that my memories would ambush me if I stepped back on the island. There were so many bad memories, sad memories, painful memories.

The last time I'd left the island, I hadn't had to stomach this heaving monstrosity; I'd been unconscious, flying beneath the thrumming helicopter blades.

Now, here I was breaking that vow all because Nate, blaspheming bastard that he'd become, had whispered Rhett's name as he died.

What the hell did that even mean? 'Rhett, not his'? Nate had called his brother Garrett by that nickname when they were young; Garrett hated it, but as far as I was aware, they hadn't spoken since Nate and I left the island. The two of them estranged; hell, we all were. I couldn't fathom what his words meant as I sat beside his death bed, and I sure as hell was no closer to working them out now.

The days between his death and the funeral were a blur. I had difficulty comprehending that the man I'd married, the fit, vibrant man was no longer with us.

The funeral was a quiet affair; I stood beside a few of his colleagues from the hospital, listening as the vicar droned on as we laid Nate to rest. An invitation to attend the reading of the will came as a surprise, and I found myself sitting numbly as Nates' Lawyer read aloud, dispersing to the waiting beneficiaries' bits and bobs, before seeing them out of his office, requesting I stay behind. Once we were alone, he took his seat behind the big wooden desk and opened a padlocked box. Slowly, one by one, he placed three items on the desktop between us. For this nightmarish crossing, a ferry ticket, a key to the family house, I had inherited my ex-husband's half of the property, and a piece of paper with the name Sonya Lawrence scrawled across it. The Lawyer apologised when I argued that I didn't wish to go back to the island but insisted these were his client's wishes. Although he wasn't privy to the reason for the travel, he'd said, 'Mr Alexander had been adamant that it was in my best interests to go'.

I hadn't wanted to do this! Feared that the incident that had occurred three years previously might come rushing back. After so many long hours sitting on my psychiatrist's

Taking extreme care, I edged along the slippery, lurching deck. Clinging, hand over hand along the rail for fear of being knocked off my feet and swept away into the unforgiving water. Grasping the metal runner on the door that would take me out of the weather and into the relative safety of the vessel, I shuffled inside. The shrieking wind instantly quieted to a low howl. Tottering along the corridor, almost dance-like as I took two steps forward, one back and swaying side to side, my hands outstretched as I tried to keep in close contact with the walls along the skinny walkway. I encountered not a soul; it appears that I was the only person silly enough to tackle the wild weather outside. Unlocking the cabin door, I gripped hold of the handle for dear life as the boat rocked back and almost set me on my arse against the opposite wall, and then the ship crested the wave and with a boom plummeted back to the raging sea, and I was thrust forward into the door. Forehead and nose struck the hard, scarred wood and tears quickly formed. I thought I glimpsed another passenger, a person, windswept and dressed in a dark hooded coat. A blast of wind gusted toward me as I attempted to regain my balance, still clinging rigidly to the door handle and swiping at the tears which clouded my vision with my free hand; finally able to see clearly, I looked again. Nobody to see, and the door at the end of the passageway shut tight against the wild elements beyond.

Stepping inside the cabin, I snapped the door closed behind me and looked in dismay at the mess. The ransacked appearance of my room had me gingerly picking my way over the clothing strewn across the floor. My suitcase, which had started this journey on the tiny pull-down table, lay open and nearly empty. No guilty thieves here, just a small ship being tossed violently on a wild ocean. Rummaging through the debris, I located my handbag and removed the small bottle of mouthwash, braced myself against the table and tipped a capful between my lips, swilling the minty liquid and spitting into a handful of tissues. Refreshed, I decided to ignore the cabins sorely needed clean-up and instead wove my way, like a drunk on a Friday night, to the safety of my bunk and thankfully sank into the deep down-filled mattress.

I lay rigid, holding tightly to the wooden sides, determined not to be thrown to the floor like my belongings and wondered how much longer this nightmare trip would take. And when we did finally land safe and sound, what kind of welcome would I receive? Would the house still be the same? One thought and the door I'd intentionally kept locked all these years flew open, and the onslaught of memories rained down on me.

I'd done my homework on the place I'd be staying. The study of its history left me excited and a little saddened. At first glance, I'd thought the two-storied villa looked out of place on the Island, much too fanciful; it would have been more suited to a property in the American South, so much so that I could envision Rhett Butler and Scarlet O'Hara on its balcony. The white walls, punctuated with coffee-coloured doors and wooden window shutters that helped shade the interior from the harsh rays of the scorching sun in the summer and to shelter the glass from the shards of gravel from the drive and surrounding fauna and flora when the seasonal winds surged, brutal and violent. A large, covered veranda encompassed the property's front and wrapped around the homesteads' right side, accessible by two large stone staircases. Picket railings between the steps, partially covered by giant palms swaying in the warm summer breeze, housed a myriad of singing cicadas.

In my minds-eye, I could picture the queues of Islander's waiting in the burning sun, as one by one, they stepped to the sheltered veranda to accept the meagre wage for hours of hard work in the property's orchards and crop fields.

That was until the raging storms desecrated the crops and uprooted the fruit trees, money became scarce, and the plantation was finally dissected and sold as small farms. The area in which the villa still sat, and surrounding acreage, was built up with structures to house endangered birdlife and small animals. The creatures were bred and raised here and then transported to the mainland to wildlife parks and sanctuaries. The endangered species program was what enticed me to the island—the need to assist with nurturing these poor creatures back from the brink of extinction.

Stopping short of the gate, I perused the magnificent plantation house, so much larger than I'd ever expected. Laughter and cajoling voices came from the other side of an eight-foot hedgerow. Moving slowly through the gate, I followed the path, trying my hardest to be quiet as I crept over the stones.

Two males, late teens, possibly early twenties at a guess, playing one-on-one basketball; feet and backs bared beneath the hot sun. Sweat ran in rivulets down their hairless bodies and soaked into the waistbands of their shorts as they dribbled the ball across the solidly packed red dirt before taking a running jump shot which had the ball rebounding with a heavy thump from the backboard straight to the opposing runner. Their laughter filled the air as they wrestled each other for the next shot.

Shyness overcame me when they turned unexpectedly and found me watching. Head bent, I stepped out, intent on walking past when two feet appeared in my line of vision, and I barely stopped in time to prevent walking into one tanned chest as the taller of the two men stood in my way.

"I'm Garrett," the one barring my escape said, "and this is my brother, Nate."

"Hey," the shorter of the two said, "What can we do for ya?"

"I err, I'm the new intern for the program," I replied, still looking at the sweat-covered muscles of Garrett's chest.

"Out the way, Rhett, let her through," Nate pulled at his brother's arm, "Dad'll be waiting for her."

"Rhett?" I squeaked, my mental image of Gone with the Wind returning as I glanced up.

"Garrett," he amended, giving his brother a menacing scowl before turning back to regard me with the deepest blue eyes I'd ever encountered; my mouth suddenly dry, breath caught in my lungs, and I knew I was in trouble!

"I err..." I coughed to find my voice and tried again. "I have an appointment at 1:15,' I glanced down at my watch, "if you could be so kind as to point me towards your father, I'd be extremely grateful."

"Up the right staircase, go in through the last door and then the second door on the left." Nate recited and thrust the ball into Garrett's stomach, "Rhett, come on, you still have two more points if you're gonna beat me, or you can forfeit, and I win, I don't care."

"Not gonna happen, little brother," Nates goading stirred Garrett into action, and they took off towards the goal, and I moved forward, climbing the right-hand set of steps following Nates' directions. As I opened the screen door, my back tingled, the hair on my forearms stood to attention, 'a ghost walking over my grave', I chanced a sneaky glance over my shoulder and found the cause; two deep blue eyes followed me, the ball bouncing aimlessly at his feet.

I came back to my bunk with those eyes still burning in my mind. The house may welcome me back, but I was damn sure Garrett wouldn't.

Garrett

Observing Addie as she manoeuvred her way back inside, I followed as closely as possible without detection. She nearly caught me when she glanced my way when an enormous wave shunted her away from her side of the corridor and threw her back into her door. I winced; damn, that must have hurt, but as much as I longed to run to her, take her in my arms and kiss away her pain, I knew it was impossible. An embrace from me would be as welcome as a pork pie at a bar mitzvah. After what I'd done, it was no surprise that she'd run.

Advancing along the passageway, I stopped beside her cabin door, wondering why she was returning to the island alone. Where was her husband? Nate had made it abundantly clear that he nor his bride would ever set foot there again.

Fate's a fickle thing! The previous crossing, on which I'd booked originally, had been cancelled due to an ongoing strike by the poorly paid wharfies. If not for the wharfies meagre wages, I wouldn't have known that Addison was returning home until she walked through my door.

Well, I could stand here and wonder all day, or I could grow a pair and ask her straight up. She was my sister-in-law, after all. I would use any excuse to be in the same room with her, and inquiring after my brother's well-being was as good an excuse as any, whether I was interested or not. I raised my hand to knock and then lowered it. What would she think of me after all these years?

I was older, wiser, and the eyes I saw in the mirror each day showed the sadness, the pain I'd been forced to endure since our last meeting. I was no longer that rash, egotistical person who loved and left, thinking only with his cock and his drinking arm. A man who realized too late what he'd let slip through his fingers.

Taking a deep breath, I raised my hand and this time, my knuckles connected with her cabin door.

Silence from the other side, was she sleeping? And then I heard her stumbling across the rocking floorboards, and the door opened.

"Yes?" she tersely asked as she took in my drenched windcheater, the black collar and hood pulled in close around my face.

Speechless, I stared down at her, a red line stood starkly against the pale skin on her forehead, and I guessed it was where she'd smacked it against the door earlier, it looked painful, and I'd hazard a guess that she may end up with more than a bit of bruising around her eyes from it.

"That looks a little painful," I pointed at her forehead, which creased into a frown as I watched, and then a grimace as her skin pulled against the swelling.

"Oh, right, yes." She replied when she realised what I was referring to. "Clumsy, I got caught off-guard by a wave," her deep green eyes slowly took in my appearance. The only area left uncovered by the windcheater was buried beneath a ragged beard; I'd not gotten around to tidying up. "Do you work on the ferry?" Maybe I did look like an old fisherman with my old jeans, steel-capped boots, and an unkempt beard. I grinned, pleased that I had the upper hand here. Until, a sharp gasp reeled my thoughts back to the moment, and I found her staring directly into my eyes, the eyes she had recognised.

"Garrett?" she whispered and visibly swallowed. The look on her face changed in an instant, and it was a look I'd hoped never to see again. Dismay, hurt, and anger flitted as she drew her shoulders back and straightened her spine.

"Hey Addie, long time," I said and pushed my way into the messy cabin before she could close the door on me; and manoeuvred my way past her clothing to the unmade bunk and sat, removing my hood to reveal the overgrown blonde hair. She was still clutching the open door when I looked up, her face reddening with rage.

We spoke simultaneously.

 "Where's that no-good husband of yours?"

"Come in, Garrett, make yourself comfortable." She spat as she slammed the door. "What are you doing here?"

With a smirk, I lay back in the bunk. Being here was such a colossal mistake, but hey, it was too late to back out now. "I believe I asked my question first." I taunted. "Where's ya husband, Addie?" I repeated.

"Ex-husband," she snapped. "And he's dead!"

I felt my face pale, and my insides begin to churn with the anger I'd buried deep all those years ago. What the hell, the bastard steals my girl and then decides he didn't want her? Wait. What? Dead?

"Did you say dead?"

She nodded, brow furrowing as she slid down the door to sit as far from me as possible in the confined cabin. "Yes, I'm sorry, Garrett, I thought you'd know."

I sat up straight and shook my head in disbelief. "I can't believe it; what happened?"

Addie shrugged her shoulders and shook her head, "I don't know. I wasn't privy to his condition. We hadn't spoken in almost a year, and then, out of the blue, I got a call from his Lawyer requesting I go to the hospital. Nate needed me to know something, Garrett, and although it makes no sense to me whatsoever, I think he wanted me to find you, possibly to explain, as your brother's final words were about you," she said as I looked on in shocked silence. "He told me I had to remember, and he said," she raised her hands' air quoting, 'He wasn't mine. Rhett isn't my ...' he never finished the sentence; he was just suddenly silent, and then he was gone."

She twisted her hands in front of her, an agitated movement she used to make when she was younger when something bothered her.

"What am I meant to remember!" she exclaimed, "and why did he say you weren't his? He was your brother! He *was* your brother, right?" she asked. Funny that she'd never asked before; after all, Nate's olive complexion and dark hair were very different from my white blonde, but the eyes gave it away. We both had my father's piercing blue eyes.

I sat silent, thinking and picturing Nate the way we used to be. We were close, closer than ordinary brothers, but there was always Dad's minor indiscretion hanging over our heads. Brother's yes, but we were brothers from different Mothers. Dad never made Nate into the dirty little secret that he could have, much to my mothers dismay. He accepted him as his son, and maybe because he'd never hidden or tried to keep secret that we had different Mums, it was never a topic for gossips.

My mum hadn't been born to island life. She missed the city and her friends, and Dad knew the only way to keep her happy was to move back to the grime filled streets, where you breathed the thick, smoggy air and worked the eight to five lifestyles of her peers. He loved Mum, would have done anything for her and their small son, but could he live and work in a city he hated? His work on the Island was so meaningful, fulfilling; Dad had never envisioned not working with the animals he saved. The day came, Mum and I left, as Dad waved farewell with promises to join us once he'd organised for Charlie Harper, his co-worker, to take over the project's running and clean up any unfinished business in the office.

After watching the ferry diminish into the distance, Dad hit the small bar and lost himself in a bottle of whiskey. I'd never seen my Dad drink; I don't recall ever seeing him with alcohol in his hand since I came back to the Island to live with him, but that night, the night we left; *that night he was about to give up all he'd been working toward; the bottle called, and he answered. Dad returned to the plantation with a belly full of malt and staggered into the office.*

Coral Harper had stayed behind to finish entering data on one of the pregnant animals when he stumbled into the room and fell across the desk, stinking drunk and sobbing his grief. Coral, their secretary, and Charlie's wife held him in her arms while he cried out the pain of losing all his life-long work, his anguished tears falling heavily onto Coral's ample chest. With a shaking hand, he had gently wiped at the wet material, fingers brushing her breast, and she'd dragged in a shocked breath which bought his face up, and then he was kissing her, and she responded wanting to help this poor broken man feel whole again. As he'd stood a while later, fingers frantically pulling his zipper closed over his spent manhood, his guilty gaze resting on the paperwork that littered the floor which minutes ago had been piled neatly on his desk. Coral stood as she shakily pulled her skirt down and, grabbing her panties, fled the room.

His unfinished business had just begun. He stayed on the Island after Coral gave him the news of her pregnancy. Charlie stood by her side until the child was born and once, he saw those spectacular blue eyes, he knew who'd fathered the tiny little boy and divorced her. Coral and my father never became an item. She struggled to bring Nate up, with most of the Island's inhabitants who had been fond of Charlie, isolating her or making snide comments, and then one day she attempted to end her life. She recovered and left the island, moved to the city, and Dad took sole custody of Nathanial, and I became his big brother.

SNAP! the sound dragged me back to the now. My attention focussed on Addie's fingers as she readied them for another snap. Visiting Dad's past, I hadn't seen her move from her perch and sway her way across on the cabin floor. A sudden wave tossed the boat, and Addie flew forward; her hand shot past my ear, and our heads collided as she fell against me. My one hand clutched at her waist in an attempt to steady her, but she crashed down on the bunk, pinning me beneath her.

"Ow," she moaned, her arm snaking up from between us to clutch at her newest injury, and tears seeped from her lowered lids, "this boat has it in for me."

"Here," I said, leaning up to press lips against her forehead, "all better."

And just like that, all thoughts flew from my mind. Addie was in my arms, her eyes staring directly into mine, and I was lost, drowning in those delicious green pools as I had for so many years of my life. Resistance in such proximity was nil as I pushed forward and captured her lips with mine.

Addison

Garrett's lips on my forehead were comforting! It was the type of thing he'd done when we first became friends; if I ever hurt myself, he'd kiss the pain away with soft lips and a smile, and I'd suddenly become a bit more accident prone, any reason for him to kiss me was fair game. This was the Garrett I loved! Before city life and the university, before he met more mature women in his study groups and dorm rooms and the popularity and conceit kicked in. And before he broke my heart! Memories flashed through my mind as I lay in his arms, the hurt, anger and loneliness, he'd taught me about all those and yet as we lay almost nose-to-nose, I knew deep down I loved him still.

It had been so long since I'd felt a soft kiss or a gentle caress, and as his hands rested against my waist and his lips claimed mine, there was no way to hide my need. With eyes closed, I pressed forward, opening for him as his tongue glided across the seam of my lips, and then there was no holding back, our mouths locked, and tongues danced.

One hand left my hip to stroke a heated trail up and down my spine, pressing the still damp dress against my heated skin, his other hand stole to my breast, and my eyes flew open. What the hell was I doing?

Thrusting my hands against his chest, I reared back, shoving myself off and away, back across the cabin with my hands outstretched as though warding him off.

"Addie, please," he begged as he sat forward, his intent clear that he was going to attempt to entice me back into his arms.

"No," I whispered and then louder. "Just NO." Reaching the door, I viciously twisted the handle and pulled it wide. "Get out."

Garrett stood, his hands scrubbed at his face before he raked them through his blonde hair and finally shook his head and moved toward me. I stood stoic, my face blank as he stopped in front of me for a mere moment. "Nate was my half-brother!" he stated, and then with a sigh, moved across the threshold. The door slammed hard, loud and final behind him, and I collapsed in a heap on the floor.

How could I not be over him? Just being in the same space made my head spin and my body scream to be touched. I couldn't endure that pain again. I just couldn't.

Slowly, methodically, I began to collect my splayed garments, stuffing them willy-nilly into my case. Clothes, toiletries, make-up, books, and an album that I hadn't opened in years, a memento of what the three of us had been to one another before life got in the way.

Giving the now clean cabin a once over to be sure I'd captured all my escaped belongings, I took a deep breath before exiting the close confines of what I'd thought to be my haven onboard. Pulling my handbag over my head and shoulder, I settled the strap snuggly between my breasts and grasped the handle of my luggage in both hands. Dragging open the door, I glanced along the passageway, checking it was empty before proceeded to sway my way to the top lounge to wait out the final hour of this infernal journey.

Casting a roving eye over my fellow travellers as they sat grasping sick bags tightly in their hands, some lying on the floor, skin-tinged green, I realized I probably wasn't looking so very different. I was relieved to note the absence of one hot, blonde, and blue-eyed Garrett. His confession bounced around in my mind. Half-brothers! How had I not known this after all the years I'd spent with both men?

As the ferry finally chugged into its destination, the engines sending vibrations throughout the deck, causing the water drops to dance; the roaring waves below us continued to crash around the hull as we rocked dangerously. My luggage bounced as I attempted to drag it behind me across the slippery wet boards, bumping my ankles and calf muscles, and I just knew they'd be black and blue by the time I reached land. Trying to roll with the ship, I impatiently waited as the passengers ahead of me swayed manically towards the decrepit looking loading ramp attached to the jetty by rope and pulleys.

As my turn came, I uttered a quiet prayer before placing my foot
on the sodden planks. Glancing fearfully at the swollen water, as it whipped into a murky foam just below the walkway, pulsing like a nightmare monster, reaching for me, trying to saturate my already cold, wet feet through the alarmingly large gaps in the ramp. I hurried the best I could, trying to reach terra firma.

The wheels on my suitcase scraped and caught in the crevices, and I finally sheathed the long handles and picked the case up, lugging it the final few meters. *Welcome back to hell*, I thought as I stood, the rain pelting like tiny bullets, stinging my skin. My hair plastered to my face and neck and my dress glued to my body, goosebumps raised like a dot-to-dot across my aching arms and my shoes squelching water.

"Miss Addison," a voice sounded through the downpour, and I squinted through the rivers of rain pouring down my face searching for its owner.

A dark-skinned man with an umbrella was hurrying along the pathway towards me.

"Oh, Miss Addison, um excuse me, Mrs Alexander," he quickly corrected himself, "my humblest apologies for my tardiness. The roads are like rivers, and traffic is horrendous."

The thought of traffic on this tiny Island being horrendous should have been enough to have me bent over in hysterics, but with my teeth chattering so hard it made my jaw ache, I was in no mood for laughter. I manoeuvred my case forward so he could grip the handle with his free hand as I took the umbrella from him to hold close above my head; the rain was drumming so loud on the thin material that it made conversation difficult.

"Th-thank you, f-for c-collecting m-me, Kemu," I shivered as he threw a coat around my shoulders, the thick padding immediately warming on my wet skin.

"No worries Miss, Mr Nate's lawyer, called last night and told me to expect you." He hurried me over the muddied stones towards the SUV, its logo splashed with mud and held open the door. Seeing me seated, he took the umbrella, shaking the drops off as much as possible and then hung it off the dash before hastening to the rear of the vehicle to deposit my luggage and then climbed into the driver's seat. He cranked the heating up and then opened the window a crack as the condensation misted the glass. With a big smile, he turned to face me, his teeth white against the darkness of his skin, and said: "Welcome home, Miss."

I jumped as the back door swung open, and the car bounced a little as Garrett climbed in behind me.

"Kemu, you old dog, trust you to let the lady in the front seat." He smiled at the older man, who just grinned back.

"She's prettier than you, Sir! Welcome home. I wasn't sure you'd be on this crossing," he replied and put the vehicle into drive and splashed his way down the worn stone road away from the dismal docks.

I could scarcely breathe, knowing Garrett sat right behind me. The kiss had knocked my senses all skew-whiff. My feelings were all aflutter; I wasn't ready to be in a confined space with him. I tuned out the conversation between the two men as they discussed the proposals to end the wharfie's strike. Turning to the window, I took in the countryside blanketed in grey as the water-laden clouds gave it a good dousing.

Pulling into the driveway, the sight of the house created a shiver, which travelled from my nape down to my tail bone. The stone steps pulled my gaze; this was where Nate had told me the incident had taken place, where I'd lost our baby, I'd tried so many times to recall the events of that night, but my psychiatrist had told me, the harder I tried, the less likely I would succeed in remembering the details. They would come when they wanted or not at all. It was unknown if the emotional trauma or the head wound I received from that night kept me in the dark.

Not waiting for Kemu or Garrett, I thrust the door wide and grabbed the umbrella, listening to the thrum of rain as I started the ascent, reaching the fifteenth of the nineteen steps I stopped. Breathing became difficult as anxiety ratcheted up a few knots. I stood still for a long moment, trying to regain my control.

"Are you Ok?" Garrett's voice close by my ear made me squeak, and I turned quickly to face him.

"I-I," I stammered and attempted another deep breath. "I don't think I can go any higher."

"You'll be fine; here, I'll help you." Garrett raised his arm; hand outstretched to grasp my shoulder, and froze as a shrill scream escaped my lips; the umbrella tumbled to the ground, bounced a little as it landed and came to rest a couple of steps down as I raised my hands to my face, cowering behind my fingers.

Garrett

What the hell just happened?

Kemu rushed up the steps taking them two at a time, nudging me out of the way as he drew closer.

"Miss Addison," he said as he drew the shaking woman's arms down and away from her face. "Miss Addison, please Miss, you're turning blue; you must breathe. Nobody is going to hurt you. Please, Miss Addison," he persisted as he patted her cheeks hard enough for it to sting, but it seemed to do the trick as she sucked in a lungful of oxygen and released it with a stuttered rattle before falling forward into Kemu's open arms and began to sob.

I stood silently on the step below and looked up at the crying woman, not understanding at all what caused the freakout. Was it the steps, had she remembered something?

"Addie," I said gently, nodding at Kemu to release the sobbing woman; his arms reluctantly dropped to his sides as he turned and strode back to the car to collect the bags and retrieved the abandoned umbrella. Addie was left standing, head bowed, shoulders heaving. "Addie, look at me, tell me what's wrong?" I yelled, fear and frustration gripping me as she just stood there.

Finally, she lifted her head, but as her gaze met mine, I was struck speechless by the absolute terror painted across her pale face.

"What?" I whispered as my eyes searched hers, "what have you remembered?"

She shook her head at me, "N...nothing, I um, it's nothing." She finished, her eyes flickering left and right to avoid looking directly at me.

"It isn't 'nothing' god-damn it. You're freaking out right now. What just happened? Talk to me."

"Why? So you can lie and hurt me all over again." Now her eyes met mine, scared yet defiant. "It was you; you were on the steps that night. It was your hand that I see in my nightmares.   Your hand that caused my baby's death!" her voice was cold, her face devoid of any colour, and it was impossible to tell if the rivulets that ran down her face was from the clouds above or her brimming eyes. The bolt of pain in my chest caught me fast and hard as the look of fear on her face was replaced by hatred. No, this wasn't happening. It wasn't my fault, not like that anyway.

"Addison, I reached for you, tried to catch you when your foot slipped. I tried, baby, I tried to save you, but I wasn't fast enough. I'm so sorry, Addie."

Addison shook her head and, turning away, began climbing the rest of the steps, stopping as she reached the summit and turned to look down on me. "I remember the darkness in your face, the anger in your eyes and your arm flying toward me. Nate said you were to blame, but he omitted to say you pushed me. And Doctor Wakefield wouldn't let him tell me more; she said I needed to remember on my own. Now I have! Stay away from me, Garrett!" And then she turned and went through the doorway.

I stood frozen to the spot as I stared after her retreating figure. What the hell, what lies had Nate fed her, what had he led her to believe?

She was right in one thing; I was angry that night!

Crazed anger swamped me when I discovered she'd married my brother on the sly.

Quietly, no family, no friends, just a couple of courthouse personnel to sign the official papers. She'd promised me the night of their disastrous engagement party that she'd put an end to their relationship.

The party! I had surprisingly, shockingly received an invite to their engagement. Should I go, or should I leave Nate and Addie be? I was still questioning my decision when I arrived on the island the day before the damned party. Maybe this was for the best; maybe now, Addison and I could finally be friends again. We could both move forward, leave the past behind and be just friends; that thought flew from my mind the moment I spied them in the garden, saw my brother drape his arm possessively across her back and bend to kiss the bared, slightly freckled skin of her shoulder. I never made it through the gateway, frozen on the spot as a jolt of pain speared my chest, winding me like some giant fist striking, stealing my breath as I watched someone else touch what was mine. Capturing my breath, I turned away. There was no way on earth that Addie and I could be just friends, and I realised at that moment, I was about to lose the one and only woman I'd ever truly loved. In my life in the city, the available women were varied, yet none of them affected me as Addie had, never touched me more profound than to lay skin to skin. Addie had penetrated my very soul, and I'd bloody stupidly pushed her away. I shoved her straight into the arms of the constantly lurking Nate, always wanting what I had. I'd been foolish. I needed to take back what was mine! I'd talk to her, tell her to wait for me while I re-organised my life, finish the business dealings and find a manager to take over the reins in the city office and then I'd come back, and I'd woo her into her rightful place, beside me, beneath me, above me. We were meant to be together.

I spent that night in the attic room of the tavern, tossing and turning as my mind conjured images of Addie and Nate together, how her hand and mouth would work him; I knew her moves, we'd learned them together, innocence lost to one another. And I knew that if I went near the homestead in my tormented state and saw the two of them, there would be blood spilt. I hadn't planned to drown my pain, but the tavern offered up the liquid relief, and as the bottle emptied, the images blurred, and numbness crept over my limbs as I fell across the bed and slept off the alcohol. I awoke late the following afternoon, my mouth dry and a rhythmic drum attacking my head. The party would be well underway, and I knew I'd missed my chance of catching Addie alone. With only a few hours till the early morning ferry left, I crawled groggily from the bed and into the shower. By 8 pm, I was clean, fed, well medicated, which I washed down with the dregs left in the bottle from the night before. I made my way toward the homestead expecting to see the party in full swing. I was surprised to discover the garden lit with coloured lights but the building in complete darkness. Half-empty plates and glasses littered the eerily silent grounds as if an apocalyptic wind had whipped through, erasing all signs of human existence. Picking my way gingerly across the lawns, I gained entrance through the back doors to be met in the littered living room by a sight I'd never forget. Smiling to myself, I watched an extremely drunk Addison, clutching a tequila bottle, swaying gently, her eyes closed, voice quavering as she sang to herself, hiccupping and slurring through the chorus.

'All by myshelf, (hic) don't wanna, (sigh) wanna, all by myshelf, anymore.'

Leaving the Island a few hours later had been the most challenging thing I'd ever done. But we'd made our promises, I would come back for her as soon as possible, and she would wait for me.

Finally returning months later, I discovered she'd not only broken her promise and married Nate but was now enormously pregnant too boot.

I'd say dark and angry was a tad mild.

"Sir, are you okay? Miss Addison?" Kemu startled me from my reverie as I found myself now staring at the empty doorframe through which Addie had stormed.

Turning to the older man with wide, shocked eyes, I responded. "Confused, Kemu. I don't understand why she would accuse me of pushing her. It's not a memory; it never happened that way, you know, you were there."

"Maybe it's time to tell her the truth, Sir."

"No, Kemu, I can't, not again. The last time I told Addie the truth, I lost everything."

Nodding sadly, he said, "I'll get the mistress settled in, Sir, and see what I can learn." Kemu readjusted his grasp on the bags as he walked past me, slowly climbing the remaining steps and disappearing through the doorway.

Feeling lost, not knowing whether I should follow them in or head back out, maybe check on the latest newborns in their nesting area, but the idea of being out in the storm wasn't appealing either. Shrugging, I began what felt like the longest climb of my life and finally entered the gloomy hallway.

She was talking loudly, down the hallway and around the corner, her voice carried as I pulled the door closed, toed the wet, muddy boots off and kicked them beneath the shoe rack. Sliding my arms from the saturated windcheater, I hung it by the hood on the back of the door next to Kemu's coat that Addie had been wearing, where it would drip and create a puddle. I knew Kemu would clean up later; that man was god-sent.

As I walked down the hall, my socks soaked up the moisture left behind from the other two. I hit the corner and paused; to reach my room, I'd need to move past Addison, and right now, I wasn't sure her seeing me was a good idea, so I stood, shifting my weight from one foot to the other, listening to the slightly heated conversation and wondering what I'd missed.

"… Mrs Alexander, the room is prep..." his voice drowned out by an insistent Addison.

"Please, Kemu, don't call me that. And this was Nate's room, and I certainly don't want to stay in it."

"But Mrs, err, Miss Addison, it was your room too before you left. I just thought …," he paused and sighed, "I'll make up a guest room for you, Miss," he amended.

"No, Kemu, not a guest room; I'll just use my old room."

I heard the pair move a little further down the passageway as Kemu attempted to sway her decision.

"It's such a small space, Miss; I'm sure you'd be more comfortable in the guest area." His voice petered out as I heard a door opening, and then came the exclamation I'd been waiting for.

"What the hell, who has been sleeping in my room?" Stepping out from my hiding place, I answered, "Yeah, that would be me, Addie," walking forward, I passed by without looking at either of them and into the room which I'd inhabited since coming home three years ago. Back then, I figured, if I couldn't have her, I'd at least sleep in her bed, live in her space and dream of times past, in her sacred den.

"What's wrong with your room? Why would you sleep in mine?" her voice was low, her anger from outside still simmering.

I shook my head at her, "go get some food while I clean my shit out," I said, still not looking at her. "Kemu, if you'd be so good as to make up my old room, I'd certainly appreciate it," I waited for his nod before closing the door on them both.

Once alone, I stared around the room realizing, I'd been living and breathing Addison for three long years. The only evidence I resided in here were my clothes hanging haphazardly from the open drawers in the old mahogany chest, an empty glass, a book which I'd barely opened and the unmade bed.

Everything else was HER!

Addison's books overflowed the bookcase, and her photographs decorated the walls. Dusty perfume bottles lived on the shelf, probably past their use-by-date, while in the closet, dresses and shoes, most likely musty and in need of throwing away, awaited her return.

The single bed adorned with a pillow, the pillow-case thin and faded from multiple washes, and the accompanying duvet cover featuring a red-haired angel in a long grey dress, her wings neatly folded back, and hands cradling a white dove; was not a manly cover, but one I hadn't the heart to change knowing her body had slept beneath it. Somehow all of these things kept her close.

Stepping to the chest, I dragged the drawers free of their mooring and tipped the unfolded clothes into a messy pile on top of the duvet. Adding my book to the stack, I quickly pulled the corners of the duvet up and tied them in a loose knot, then dragged it along the floor to the door. Turning back to the bed, I tore the sheet from the mattress and stuffed it inside the pillowcase and slipped it beneath my arm, grabbed the glass and strode across the room, opened the door and lifted my gypsy bundle of belongings then without a backwards glance I left Addison's room. I didn't need to linger; the need to be in her room so I could be close to her was no longer there; there was something better in the house now, the real deal. Addie was back!

Addison

Glaring at the closed door, I felt Kemu's hand touch my arm. "Come on, Miss. I'll walk you to the kitchen before preparing Mr Garrett's room." I didn't need 'walking' anywhere; I knew the way, but I followed, feeling like a zombie, and strangely enough, it was Kemu's brain that I needed to digest. I was sure he'd have the answers I so desperately required. Meanwhile, inside my head, my thoughts were like a balloon blown up and let go, careening fast and uncontrollable, not allowing me to get a grasp on any one of them.

What the hell was Garrett's deal? Why on earth would he hole up in my old room when his was twice the size and housed all the creature comforts? In by-gone years, all three of us had spent vast amounts of time in there, gaming on the play-station, watching movies on the large wall-mounted screen, and drinking the cheap whiskey that Nate always managed to procure, I never did find out from where. My room, in comparison, had been a mere broom closet, so why was Garrett camping out there? Come to think of it, what was he doing here at all? I was sure Nate had said the place had a manager. Garret lived in the city, didn't he? Was he married? And if so, did she know about me, about Nate? Had Garrett confessed how he'd caused the death of his brother's child and ruined our lives?

I suddenly realized I'd assumed an awful lot over the last couple of years, coming back here to find all my assumptions were just that.

"I'll leave you to it, Miss," Kemu said and disappeared out the side door before I could stop him. So much for picking his brains.

Autopilot clicked in as I filled and switched on the kettle; my fingertips sought the correct cupboard for the mugs, the coffee and sugar homed where they'd always been. Soon I stood sipping the vital, black elixir of life, the scalding liquid burning a trail across my tongue and down my throat. The much-needed caffeine punch was just what I needed to warm my still shivering body and bring some clarity back to my mind.

Leaning back against the cabinets with my hands wrapped around the mug, I surveyed the kitchen. It seemed nothing had changed, the massive block of wood Kemu used for chopping had more knife scars, and the potted herbs along the bench below the window were bushier at their base as if snipped with scissors instead of being harvested regularly by hand. Not a dish out of place, no food prep on the benches, Kemu certainly kept this space clean as a whistle.

Standing alone in the kitchen, my coffee warming both my insides and out, the clothes drip-drying on my body was not the homecoming I'd expected. A door slammed somewhere in the homestead, making me jump. Swilling the dregs down the sink and placing my mug in the dishwasher, I retraced my steps back to the bedroom, grasped the handle of my suitcase and levered it from where it had been left in the hallway and entered my old domain. Garrett had removed all signs of his being here; except, I walked to the bedside cabinet, my fingers moving of their own accord to the sticky ring left behind by Garrett's glass. Bringing my fingertips to my nose and inhaling, the scent of whiskey filled my nostrils. How often did the man drink himself to sleep? I found the question made me sad. Where did we all go wrong? How did we wind up bitter, angry, lonely, and sad?

Wiping my fingers down my still damp dress to remove the sticky residue, I bent to open my case and rummaged through the mess of clothing and dragged out some underwear, a pair of mottled green leggings and a baggy, long-sleeved shirt. Digging a little deeper, I discovered my toilet bag, which still held at least half of my toiletries; the rest, of course, were dispersed throughout my luggage where I'd thrown them back on the ferry crossing from hell and left the room. The thought of taking a nice, long, hot shower made me smile; a memory of Nate, back when things were good popped to mind, *"a long hot shower, it's just what the doctor ordered,"* he'd say with a grin, *"should I write you a prescription?"* My smile faded to realise that Nate wouldn't be writing any more scripts. He was gone. I turned the shower dial until the little black arrow pointed midway red; I knew it would be too hot to stand under for long; but I needed to feel the heat prickle my skin, to bring some sensation back, and chase away the numbness that existed within my body. I shucked the creased material from my shoulders, and the dress pooled around my feet as I quickly unhooked my bra and stripped out of my remaining garments, leaving everything where they fell. Cringing a little as I stepped into the scorching stream, I slid the glass door closed, and the steam quickly engulfed me. I stood for as long as I could beneath the intense heat, breasts, belly and legs turning a bright shade of red as my skin burned, my scorched skin itched. I finally gave in and moved the dial to a more comfortable temperature and ducked my head beneath the calming waterfall, and stood, allowing the water to wash my pain down the drain, if only momentarily. I was home, and I felt an easy peace settle over me.

Loud banging roused me from my deliciously warm stupor, and Garrett's voice from beyond the door calling out, "You still alive in there? Leave us some hot water!" I realized I'd nodded a little, dozing whilst still standing; horses and cows did it, so why not us humans? With pruned fingertips, I quickly lathered my hair and then my body and allowed the bubbles to disperse as the droplets of water broke them down and chased them away. Turning the water off, I stepped from the steamed enclosure to the slightly less steamy bathroom. Wrapping a large fluffy towel around my reddened body, I quickly pulled my toothbrush out and scrubbed my teeth, feeling so much fresher, the mouth wash had helped back on the boat, but there was no better feeling than freshly brushed teeth. Another knock on the door, "Addie, come on," then a barely heard muttering, "bloody women and their bathroom hogging." It made me grin, but I decided maybe he was right; I'd been in here way too long. Damn it all, the clean clothing I'd planned on wearing was now damp. A quick check to be sure the towel covered everything it should, I bundled the dirty clothes and dropped them in the hamper and then clutching my clean clothing opened the door, and came face to face with Garrett, literally, as he rested his head on the forearm leaning on the door jamb. "Thought you'd slipped down the bloody plughole," he griped and then sucked in a breath as he realized I was clad only in a towel.

His eyes dropped from my face, glancing to where the reddened skin rose and fell above the rough, damp material and released that held breath, blowing cold air across my burning chest. I couldn't take my eyes from his face as I catalogued the emotions flitting across it. The heat in his gaze slightly glazed as he ogled the swell of my breast cast upward by my arm crossed beneath them to keep the towel in place. His breathing quickened, blowing another cold rush across my prickling skin, cooling, soothing the burn and pebbling my nipples beneath the damp towel. It seems the feelings I'd buried deep for the last five years hadn't died like I imagined they would; he still affected my body even as my mind rebelled with the hurt and desolation he'd caused in my life. I watched numbly as the hand by his side rose slowly, and his fingertips traced a tingling current across my flesh, feeling the heat emanating from where the too hot water had boiled the blood beneath. Now it was my turn to suck in my breath as he moved, like a striking cobra; both hands gripped my shoulders, bringing his face close to mine, his eyes no longer glazed with lust and wanting but raw with need and, wait, was that anger? "What the hell have you done, silly girl?" with a quick shake of my shoulders, he released me; as my clothes dropped and I was left clutching at the slipping towel, he moved me to one side and stormed into the misty bathroom and yanked open the cabinet door. Seizing a bottle of cooling lotion, he scanned the label and nodded before turning back and thrusting the bottle at me. "Here, this will help cool the burn. Get dressed. We'll talk when I've showered," and with that, he closed the door in my face. I poked my tongue childishly at the door and bent to retrieve my dropped bundle before stalking down the hallway to my room and closing the door. Throwing the clothes at the bed and letting the towel fall, I proceeded to do as ordered, soothing the lotion over the reddened skin and wishing the gentle touch of fingertips belonged to the work-roughened hands of Garrett.

Garrett

Hell! I was in so much trouble right now. Addie was Aphrodite re-incarnate. She was a goddess, love, sex, and beauty wrapped in her white covering, and I was damned! The want! The need! The lust that rose to tent my trousers all proclaiming my feelings for the one woman I lost. My brother, barely cold in his grave and I was ready to take back what he stole from me.

I wiped the mirror clear of steam and stared at the blurred, bearded face in the glass. It was no wonder Addison hadn't recognized me straight away onboard the ferry; I don't think my own family would have known the scruffy wretch I'd become. The last three years, since taking up permanent residency on the island, alone in the house, except for Kemu, who lived in a self-contained flat, housed above the garages at the rear of the property, I'd let myself go.

Shaking my head in disgust at my sad reflection, I bent and dragged open the bottom drawer and withdrew a pair of scissors and my razor. Within minutes, the water-filled basin was awash with scratchy bristles as I snipped the coarse hair from my chin and cheeks. Satisfied that it was as short as I could get it, I squirted foam into my palm and slathered my face in white before dragging the razor down my jawline and rinsing the whisker-filled foam from the blade. Over and over, my skin was reddening and become tender with each scrape until finally, my naked face stared

back at me. The once golden tanned skin was a sallow off white where the sun hadn't been able to penetrate the thick hair but taking the beard had also taken the age from my face, except for the eyes. The deep blue was like a lens into my tortured soul, the pain radiating from within. I turned away from the image and, stripping down, moved into the glassed stall. Flipping the faucet, I gasped as the cold shower spray hit my body, and I stood shivering until the heat finally began to build and my body relaxed into the warm water; sadly, my mind refused to do the same. Sometime later, as drops rained down my cheeks, I was unsure if they were tears or the now chilled spray; as the water began to run colder, I turned the water off, and grabbing a towel, held it to my face in an attempt to muffle the sound of my sobbing. I was a grown man, for Christ's sake, and here I stood, bawling like a toddler. Why? Was it the return of Addie to the place where everything that was right went wrong? Or was it because my brother was dead and that he'd died without fixing our relationship? Sobs slowing, I thought back to the telegram that Kemu handed me after Addie was safely behind closed doors in her room, notifying me of Nate's death, a follow up to the phone call I'd missed due to the ferrymen strikes. Kemu had taken the call from Nate's lawyer; that's how he knew Addie would be sailing. The words on that slip of paper burned in my mind. So cold, so final.
MR NATHANIAL ALEXANDER: DECEASED.
WILL READING: CONCLUDED

MRS ADDISON ALEXANDER ARRIVING: 15 JUNE
TRANSCRIPT OF THE READING: TO FOLLOW.

Taking a long, deep inhale, my lungs inflated to total capacity as I slowly counted to five and then released the breath in a slow, steady stream. Turning my back so I wouldn't catch sight of the teary man in the mirror. I wrapped the towel around my still damp hips and opened the door. With shoulders back and head held high, determination in my stride, I turned toward my room, leaving behind the bearded wretch and the broken man of the last three years in the steam-filled room.

Throwing on the first pair of black jeans and an old colour-worn t-shirt, plucked from my newly placed wardrobe, a pile in the centre of the bed; I realized I'd have to fill the drawers before I was sleeping tonight. I bet Addie had already unpacked her bags and filled the empty spaces I'd left behind in my mad dash to remove my stuff from her room. Strange that she would want that old, cramped room back when as Nate's wife, ex-wife, I corrected myself, could have had the roomier space she'd shared with her husband. Maybe she didn't want to remember the good times since things had turned sour between them. I wondered what the hell had gone wrong? Hopefully, I was about to find out all I'd missed since our last encounter.

My bare feet padded along the wooden planks, automatically manoeuvring myself around the creaky boards and entered the living room silently, stalling just inside the door to appreciate the view I'd never expected to see again. Addison lounged on the soft sofa, her body sinking deep into the blue cushions, her head fallen back, so the red of her hair contrasted greatly against the dark headrest. Her eyes were closed, and her chest lifted and fell with her gentle breaths. Addie was beautiful, her jaw relaxed as she slept, and a soft snore escaped from between her parted lips. The poor woman must have been exhausted from the ferry ride, and God only knew what she had endured since Nate's death, and maybe even further back than that. What had happened with their marriage? Why had nobody told him that they'd separated? Was Nate cheating with another woman? Or, and this thought rocked his socks, maybe Addie had strayed, was there another man? He couldn't bear it; the idea of her with his brother had nearly killed him, but to think of her with another man in her life, in her bed, would undoubtedly be the end of him. It would be difficult enough to establish himself back in her life, with the ghost of the lost child between them. The memories, or rather her lack of memories, and Nate's words of blame were going to be a battle.

He tiptoed forward and, with great care not to nudge her, sat as close as he could to the sleeping woman. Yes, he had questions; they needed to talk, but right now, just being close to her after all this time, being able to look upon her sleeping form would be enough; he'd waited this long, what was another few minutes while the woman of his dreams caught a few moments of rest. He'd happily sit here and wait.

Addison

'The taste of whiskey, bittersweet, overpowered the fading tang of tequila as his tongue slid against mine. He tasted so good, the feeling sublime. Cold hands scorched my heated skin. His touch tormented my over-stimulated nerve endings, and my alcohol saturated brain gave in to what my normal level-headedness wouldn't. It let him in!

I moaned into his mouth as his tongue continued its lazy suckling of my own, and my lady parts wetted in anticipation of what this mouth could do. His body blanketed mine, and as he pressed forward, joining our bodies once more, marking me as his own, as his once gentle thrusting increased, growing more manic. Our panting breaths mingled …

I glowered up at the man I loved and hated. Anger and disbelief were suffocating my mind. "You promised you'd wait for me," he hissed, the fury on his face frightening.

"Wait, what?" my voice shrill, "What do you mean, 'I promised you?' You abandoned me two years ago, left me here to suffer alone; you loved me, but not enough. I was never enough!

I was naïve for a long time, blinded by my feelings for you." A sob erupted, the sense of loneliness swamping me, dragging me back down. "You were my first love, we were everything to each other, or so I thought."

"Two years?" he raged back, "I came back to stop you from marrying my brother."

My hand caressed my swollen belly; the baby kicked as if our yelling had woken it from its watery slumber.

"No," I whispered, "I waited for you...."

"Don't be angry," I begged, "please listen." A hand raised, my head snapped back as Garrett struck and through blurred tears, his face morphed, and Nate's angry eyes glared down at me, his fist clenched. I screamed and shrank back as his arms came up and grasped my shoulders. My arms flailed as I attempted to bat him away as he began to shake my body.

"Addie, wake up, for God's sake, woman. Wake up." My lids snapped open and met not the light blue eyes of my ex-husband but the gorgeous blue of the man who haunted my dreams and visited my nightmares. "What the hell, honey, one minute you're groaning like your, well, like I remember you groaning and the next your fighting for your life, screaming like a banshee. Who were you fighting, Addie?"

Frowning as the dream slowly trickled into obscurity, I knew it was the same dream turned nightmare, but everything became a muddied mess each time I attempted to analyse it. Nothing seemed to fit.

I raised my hand, fingers touching my cheek, feeling the ghostly tingle of fingerprints where the dream strike had landed. Still only half awake, my thoughts tumbled within my head as my eyes slid closed again, sleep tugging at me.

"Addie, wake up. Who were you fighting?"

"You hit me! You were so angry! Please don't be angry?" I murmured.

"No, honey, I just shook you awake. Was someone hurting you? Tell me, who hit you, who were you dreaming of?" Garrett's eyes flashed; how dare someone lay a hand on his woman.

"You, you were here. No! Wait, I was angry because you weren't here, and Nate...." I was so confused, I yawned and cracked my lids slightly, blinking. I was so tired.

"Nate, what, Addie? Nate hit you?"

I swallowed hard and closed my eyes. "It-it was a dream; it's gone now," I mumbled, trying to force my eyelids to cooperate and stay open. Garrett held my shoulders, his thumbs gently caressing as they stroked back and forth, his gaze though was stern as he studied me, and for a moment, I felt like I was on a slide beneath a microscope; I needed to move before he read too much. Shaking myself free of his hand, I shuffled sideways along the couch, putting distance between us. The corner cushions sent chills along my skin, snagging the throw-rug folded on the armrest; I covered myself, hiding beneath its bulk, all the time fighting to conceal the tiny fragments of my dream from him. I needed time to analyse them myself before having to share them with him. But shutting Garrett down wasn't going to be that easy.

"Who hit you, Addison?" The commanding tone in his voice was unmistakable; he didn't intend to let this drop.

"Please, Garrett, leave it be; it was just a dream."

"But it wasn't, was it? The look on your face, the scream, the way your fingers touched your cheek; this time, it may have been in a dream, but it wasn't always so, was it? Someone hit you! And you're going to tell me all about it." He stood swiftly, making me jump and press back even deeper into the cushions and his eyes grew darker still. "I'm sorry, I didn't mean to startle you," he apologised, then added, "your reaction right there tells me I'm right." He moved across to the cabinet and poured whiskey into two glasses, bringing them back to where I sat; he handed one to me before sitting and gulping his back in one shot. I sipped at mine, allowing the amber liquid to slide along my tongue, feeling the tingling tickle as it warmed my throat before pooling, scorching within my chest.

I had to give him something, what to say, what not to say, where to begin? With a deep breath and a long sigh, I twisted in my seat to face him.

"I left Nate, not the other way around," I stated. "Your brother was an angry man, from the moment I said, 'yes' to his proposal, he changed somehow." I frowned a little, trying to pinpoint the reasoning for the change as I had so many times before. "But I still married him, so I guess that's on me, right?" The nerve in his jaw ticked, fury flashed in his eyes, but he stayed quiet, his eyes never leaving my face. Realising a response was not forthcoming, I continued. "We had an engagement party, but you knew that already because you received an invite." I glanced away and took another swig from my glass. Still no response. "You, you never came, but Nate found me standing at the dock waiting for you, long after the last person had disembarked the last ferry. I'd been there most of the day, whilst he'd been organising the party; he'd thought my absence was due to readying myself, hair, nails etc. But I hadn't been! I was waiting for you, waiting so I could explain, so I could," I stopped and looked away, knowing how pitiful I sounded. His fingers came into view as he hooked them beneath my chin and turned me back to face him.

"What?" he said softly, "so you could what?"

I swallowed hard and pushed his hand away. "So I could assure myself that we were truly over. I didn't want to marry Nate if there was still a chance that you, that we, weren't finished. I guess I never really let you go. I always thought that maybe?' I shook my head as I tried to focus on the story I'd never told anyone. "Nate was furious when he found me, hauled me back to the house and demanded I get ready to face our guests, and when I tried to explain to him, he slapped me. Half an hour later, the imprint of his fingers hidden beneath my make-up, he put his arm around my shoulders, and our guests cheered and toasted, 'to the happy couple'; it was as if the slap never happened. I played the happy hostess, drank champagne, laughed, talked and then drank some more to forget, forget the pain from that strike and worse, to dull the ache as I finally accepted that you weren't ever coming back for me."

I stopped and raised the glass to my lips, threw back what was left and handed the empty tumbler back to Garrett, who silently rose, walked to the cabinet and refilled both our drinks. Handing mine back to me, he sat again, his face furious, eyes blazing.

"So it was Nate in your dream. He hit you the day of your party! But it wasn't the only time, was it?"

I slowly shook my head. No. It wasn't the only time.

"He did seem genuinely sorry. It didn't happen again, not until, well, not until I lost the baby. After that, he was never the same again, always angry. I thought it was his way of dealing with the grief of losing our child, yet he never seemed to be sad, just filled with a bubbling fury that never seemed to diminish. Sometimes he'd leave, for days at a time, I never knew where he went, but it was a relief when Nate went away, although when he returned if anything, his anger intensified." I paused, the rest was too personal to share, so I finished by simply adding. "And so, I left him."

"After how long, Addie. How long did you put up with his abuse?" he asked through clenched teeth.

"Two years," I mumbled. And then, a little louder, I answered. "Two years I stayed, I felt I owed Nate, and I needed someone solid. We lived with a ghost between us; any feelings he had for me seemed lost along with the baby. But I clung to him; he was an anchor, my mind was adrift on a swirling ocean, each wave promising a memory to be retrieved, but the more I swam towards it, the further it receded. Nate was my rock; even if his edges were cruelly sharp, he was the only solid thing in my life whilst I was floating.

Enough about me. Catch me up on what you've been doing over the last three years." Bringing the glass to my lips, I knocked back the whiskey before climbing from the seat to refill the tumbler again. I couldn't be too close to him, with him studying my every emotion, every reaction on hearing his story. I wasn't a good enough actress to hide the hurt if he was to tell me he'd met his soulmate and been happily married whilst I'd been living in misery. Uncapping and tipping the bottle, I watched as the golden liquid escaped the confines of its long-standing prison, only to be caught in the waiting tumbler. A moment of unasked for freedom and then with one gulp, you're locked away in an acidic cell, forgotten. *Had I been a shot of whiskey? Protected within Garrett's glass barrier through my late teens, watching the world from behind that shield, safe and loved, until that fateful day when he uncapped the bottle and poured me away, giving me the freedom I never wanted?*

"Nothing to tell." Garrett's voice in my ear made me jump, spilling some of the drink I was still pouring. "You gonna leave some of that for me?" he asked, eyeing my half-filled glass, then taking the bottle from my hand; he measured the same amount into his tumbler.

My heart pounded in my chest, I'd not heard him leave his seat, and now, he was close, too close. If I were to turn, we would be touching, knew from past close encounters that I'd have to tip my head back, to look up at his handsome face, the movement an open invitation for him to lower his head, I stood still. His breath whispered against my ear as he murmured, "I came home, Addie. And I stayed. Alone! I took your room, lay in your bed, slept on your pillow every night."

I watched his hands, remembering how those long fingers had pleasured every inch of my skin. Placing his glass next to mine, he shifted, moving his hands to my hips as his lips nuzzled my neck and whispered. "Is that what you wanted to hear?"

A strangled sob fought its way to freedom, and the next instant, a wash of tears adorned my cheeks. Silent now, he turned my body and peppered tiny kisses atop the dampness on my skin. It was too much, I couldn't keep what I was feeling from showing in my eyes, so I buried my face in his chest and hid whilst I cried. Strong arms encompassed me, dragging me closer, hands gently stroking up and down, calming and cradling all in one. I wasn't the only one who had been lonely; he hadn't moved on either. Long minutes later, I raised my face, eyes searching out his, and what I found hidden in the deep blue depth was a punch to the chest, like a giant fist pressing, pushing the breath from my lungs, and stolen by Garrett's lips as they claimed mine in a searing kiss.

Swooning just a little, I held on tight, my fingers clenching his shirt as I fought and won against the tiny gap, which was still far too wide between our bodies. I pressed myself against him, needing the contact, feeding my soul with the only person ever to assuage my hunger.

In my mind, I knew this was all too good to be real, I was still dreaming, damn it all, this one felt more real than all the others, I knew I'd awaken, and I would imminently feel the loss, as I had every other time, I'd dreamt of holding Garrett. Clutching tighter, I held on, relishing the feel, yet knowing soon, the dream would turn to nightmares, and he'd be gone once more.

Garrett

The salty taste of her tears on my tongue as I lay butterfly kisses on her face made the ache to hold her intolerable. I wasn't strong enough to give her time, I needed to mend the broken fences of our friendship and rebuild the fortress that once housed the love we had for one another, and it needed doing now. My arms snaked around her, pulling her close, holding her as she cried. Oh, I'd missed the feel of her heart beating, the warmth of her body beneath my palms. Doctors' rules be damned, she needed to learn the truth, and maybe the way to help her regain what she'd lost in memory was to relive some of it. I'd lost so much, been so lonely, missed her every minute of every day. When she finally pulled back from my chest, I panicked, thinking she'd retreat into her angry shell, but instead, she raised her head, and her green eyes sought out and locked with mine. I took a chance and leant forward, my lips caught hers, and the world spun. I wasn't just hungry for her. I was starving, the want, the need swamped any rational thought as I feasted at her mouth; nipping and nibbling, caressing and tasting, and as her hands lifted from my shirt, to manoeuvre my face to deepen the kiss yet further, I thought I'd died and gone to heaven. Was she still in love with me? Could she forgive and put the awful past behind her?

Addie pulled back first, gasping for breath. I released her lips but held tight to her soft curves. "You taste like whiskey! Damn, I'm still dreaming." She whispered against my mouth.

"Mmm, so do you," I said softly. "Last time we kissed in this room, we had a whiskey, tequila mash-up."

Addie froze, "What? What did you say? Tequila?"

"Yes. Remember?" I frowned down at her, "I kissed you, and since you'd drunk over half the bottle, you tasted like tequila. You were an extremely cute drunk; I was quite hypnotized watching you sing and sway, a concert just for me."

A confused frown appeared on her brow as her hands stroked my cheeks, fingertips grazing across my lips and over my chin. "You had a beard. Damn it; I am still dreaming," the words uttered low, talking to herself. Then without pause, her left hand moved, and I watched in dismay as she pinched herself hard.

"Ouch." She squealed, and she looked at me with such confusion swirling in her eyes, "I'm awake! But this isn't real." She shook her head.

"It's real, babe, I'm here, talk to me," I coaxed; that uncertainty in her eyes scared me. What the hell was going on in that head of hers? Why would she still think she was dreaming? Were her memories returning? Maybe it was all too much, too fast; she seemed to be confused about something.

She opened her mouth, closed it, and opened it again and began to sing. "All by myself, don't wanna be, all by …."

"Yeah, Addie, that's the song. You were singing it the night of your engagement party, remember?"

"James Page died." She muttered; her eyes opened wide. "How could I have forgotten that?"

"Yes, Jimmy died, but what has your singing got to do with that? Addison, you're not making sense."

"I was singing 'cos I was alone, they all left me. The engagement party was a farce anyway, I certainly wasn't feeling it, and with a call from the hospital, it shut down pretty quickly. James had coded. He was one of Nate's patients, his operation had gone fine, and he was doing great, and then, well, he wasn't. Everyone loved James, and with over half the Island's inhabitants here at the party when the call came, they all beelined for the hospital right along with Nate; and I stayed here, alone, standing amongst the dregs of an event that was a lie. That tequila bottle was my companion that night, and whilst I selfishly drank myself into oblivion, James died.

I don't even recall Nate coming home; the tequila ambushed my brain." She shook her head as if trying to clear the fog the tequila had caused that night, "I have trouble recalling it, everything is so confusing, and yet the dream I had that night, it's always with me, I dream it repeatedly before it morphs into my nightmare.

It felt so real, Garrett, but I know it's a dream and not memory because you featured in it."

I grinned at that, "So you dreamt about me," I said, wiggling my eyebrows at her, "It must have been a doozy if it's re-occurring. Care to share?"

She blushed, the colour deepening as I watched her sift through her thoughts, and I knew she wasn't going to give me the dream in its entirety. "I err, I dreamt that you came home the night of the party to stop me from marrying Nate." She shrugged.

I stared at her, shocked. "Addison, I did come home that night. You weren't dreaming! I found you here alone, as you said, surrounded by dirty glasses and plates. Drunk as a skunk, that tequila bottle took quite a hit. I made coffee, we talked, and you promised to call off the engagement and wait for me." I stopped talking and stepped back. "But you didn't wait, Addie! When I finally came home for good, months later, you were married, and I was so fucking furious. I'd spent all that time wrapping up the loose ends in the city so I could get back and start a new life with you, and it had all been for nothing."

"No," she whispered, her eyes filled with pained anguish. "It was a dream. It had to be. We were together," she blushed again, "physically together, and I dreamt that I lay in your arms and slept. But it wasn't real. It couldn't have been because I woke up, Garrett, and it wasn't your arms that held me as I'd believed; they were Nates."

Holy shit! Somewhere between the time I'd crawled from her bed and boarded the early ferry back to the city and her waking up, Nate had arrived home and climbed in beside her. No wonder she was confused. Hell, she'd probably had the worst hang-over ever, which was why the dream scenario was so easy for her to believe. I wanted to throw my head back and howl at the unfairness of the entire situation. All these years, alone, angry at her, at myself, when the real blame lay with half a bottle of tequila. The rest, pure circumstance.

Reaching around her for my half-filled glass of whiskey, I chugged it, feeling the burn down my throat before forming a scorching pool in my chest.

It was all too much! Anger ignited as it had three years ago, and I hurled the glass toward the brick fireplace, watching as it shattered to a million pieces on the hearth; the shining shards capturing the setting sun which had finally fought its way from behind the heavy clouds, now that's an analogy if ever there was one.

Addison

I watched the crystal glass shatter, just as my life had shattered four years ago when I'd awoken in the arms of Nate.

I woke slowly, not my usual, eyes open, jump out of bed type of morning. No, this morning, my eyes didn't want to open at all, didn't want to let go of the beautiful dream, but open them, I did. Slithers of light attacked my retinas as I cranked my eyelids into slits, and the dream slipped away as I groaned, 'so bright'. If it hadn't been for my bladder screaming 'empty me' through painful pressure, I would have shut out the glare and huddled the day away in the warm, safe cocoon beneath the heavy blanket. Too heavy! Its lead-like weight pressing into my skin was extreme, wrapping itself around me, pinning me in place. And then it hit me. I wasn't alone! The weightiness belonged to an arm thrown across my belly, holding me, pressing my back against a warm, hard body. Oh-my-God, it hadn't been a dream; he was here. With exaggerated care so as not to awaken Garrett, I twisted my neck and peered over my shoulder, and froze. Nate lay sleeping, head resting on my pillow. It was his heated skin that enveloped my naked body, his arm weighing down the blanket and increasing my need to pee. With a slow, snake-like wriggle, my feet dropped soundlessly to the floor while I gently eased his arm to the mattress. Then keeping a close watch on his face, careful not to wake him, I stood and tip-toed silently, backwards to the door, where I snagged the dressing gown from its hook and hugged it tightly to my chest, before slipping out of the room and making a beeline for the bathroom.

Pulling the material around my shoulders, I cringed at the reflection in the mirror, make-up smudged eyes stared back, and with my bandit's mask and my cloak-like covering, I looked like a hung-over superhero. Dropping down to sit on the toilet, bony elbows digging into my thighs, I closed my eyes and placed my aching head in my hands and released a slight trickle. I hissed at the tenderness between my thighs and sat bolt upright, the pain in my head kicking up a notch, and yet it was the ache in my nether regions which now held my attention. 'What had I done? After all these months, putting off having sex with Nate, insisting we wait until we were married, and I'd stupidly slept with him whilst I was drunk. The dream? Oh, no, I didn't! I shook my head and instantly regretted it. Maybe I deserved the pain. Guilt engulfed me as the realization sank in; while I'd been having sex with Nate's body, in my mind, I had been making love with his brother. What sort of woman does things like that? That beautiful dream of Garrett and our lovemaking was a drunken fantasy. Nate deserved better!

I didn't remember him coming home or him climbing into my bed. Tears gathered and dripped onto my thighs. Garrett's homecoming and lovemaking may have been a dream, but the toilet tissue I patted between my legs;

showed proof that the intimate act had been genuine; it just happened to be with the wrong brother.

Moments later, with my forehead resting against the wall, the showerhead rained lukewarm water on my neck and shoulders, my headache beating a relentless drum mirroring the constant thrum of my heartbeat. I felt bereft; my having sex with Nate was the final nail in the coffin, hopes of Garrett and my reconciliation, dead. The place in my heart where Garrett resided felt empty because of my betrayal, and the more I thought of what I'd done, the more that dark, vacant space filled with guilt. How could I face Nate? How does one look a man, used to fulfil a fantasy based on another person, in the eye?

A knock at the bathroom door made me jump, my arm bumping the shelf and sending the bottles of gel and shampoo cascading to the floor with a loud, vibrating boom. I winced; the noise was far too loud for my pounding head.

"You okay, Addison?" Nate's concerned voice rang through the closed door.

"Fine, I'm just fine," I called back. "Knocked the shelf is all."

"Right, just letting you know, I've made coffee, so don't be too long, or it'll be cold."

"Thanks, I'll be right out."

Shit! I thought I'd have had more time to compose myself. Why was he up so damn early? Towelling dry, I shrugged into my overly large dressing gown and tugged the belt tight around my middle. Clearing a circle on the fogged mirror, I gazed at my slightly contorted self in the smeary glass, searching for the guilt I had painted on my face. To my surprise, I looked the same as always, strange how the outer shell could hide a mountain of turmoil. Quickly finger combing my hair into place, I left the safe confines of the bathroom and headed to the kitchen. I had to face Nate at some stage; it may as well be sooner than later.

"Morning, Sweetheart," he said as I entered the room and headed straight for the steaming coffee on the table. I straddled the bench seat and wrapped shaking fingers around the hot mug, took a sip and groaned in appreciation. Nate sidled behind me, arms wrapping around my waist as he nuzzled into my neck. "I saw you hit the tequila last night. Glad someone had a good time," he whispered.

Oh, no, maybe the sex had been bad if I was the only one to have had a good time.

"I'm sorry I was in such a mess when I came home; losing Jimmy like that has completely thrown me."

Did Jimmy die? That is so sad!

"I really appreciate that you let me stay with you; it was a hard night." Oh, he'd been hard alright, and the ache I was experiencing right now told me just how hard. So that's what had happened; it had been a pity fuck. The guilt just kept piling up.

Steering the conversation away from the events after he got home, I figured it was safer to discuss poor Jimmy instead. "So, what happened at the hospital?"

And that was all it took. Nate moved away and started talking, thinking out loud as he moved around the kitchen collecting ingredients, beating eggs, grating cheese, chopping ham, as I simply sat and let the sounds wash over me, tuning in to my thoughts.

I jumped when a plate laden with an omelette and toast banged onto the table in front of me, followed by his plate as he took the seat opposite and quickly chewed down a few bites.

"So, what do you think, should we?" he asked.

Uh-oh, what had he been saying? "Um, y-yes," I stammered, my voice rising a little at the end of the word as if making a question of my own since I wasn't at all sure what I agreed to but hoped it was the correct answer. The smile that lit his face told me it was the answer he was after, but what had I just said 'yes' too?

"Great," he said, leaning across the table and placing a gentle kiss on my lips, "I'll organise a couple of witnesses, and all you have to do is find a pretty dress to wear."

Huh? What?

"Damn shame the registry office is closed today. If Jimmy's death has taught me anything, it's just how quickly life can change, and I don't want to wait for a second longer than I have to in becoming your husband." And with that said, he

strode from the room, leaving me open-mouthed and wondering what the hell just happened.

The following day, dressed in a white, flowing sundress and holding a simple sprig of heather, I mounted the steps to the registry office. My brain was a whirlwind; my head still ached from my over-indulgence of tequila from Saturday night, the dream I had of Garrett playing on repeat in my head, over and over, wishing for a different outcome. However, I always woke to Nate's face beside me on the pillow. I shouldn't be marrying Nate; it was wrong considering every time I closed my eyes, it was his brother's face that I saw, yet the guilt this caused me was overpowering, and I felt I owed him somehow. Maybe getting married was the only way I could stop hankering for what I would never have. The double doors of the registry office banged closed behind me that Monday morning, shutting out the bright sunlight and the sky, so blue it resembled Garrett's eyes. Internally I closed the metaphorical door, shutting Garrett away, locking and pocketing the key, before turning a strained smile toward the two witnesses, the registrar and my husband-to-be and repeated the sacred vows. "I do."

"I do," Garrett said.

"Huh, what? Sorry!" *I was miles away, lost in the past.*

"I was just saying we could both do with some food," he said, kneeling at the hearth and brushing the slithers of crystal onto the dustpan. "Go find some shoes; we can eat at the pub. They still do a mean steak and fries."

He was right, my stomach gurgled, and the whiskey was hitting me way too hard; I could do with a feed. Leaving him to capture the wayward shards of glass, I went in search of a dry pair of shoes. My wardrobe still held several dresses, the smell of them mildewy, and I was reasonably sure they'd wind up in the ragbag, and below them, on the floor, lined up like soldiers were my slip-on canvas shoes, ranging in colours, a pair to match each outfit. Not sexy, slinky high heels, all flats since heels were hopeless on the island, where most people went barefoot or wore crocs, but I drew the line at that; rubber shoes with holes, I don't think so. Pulling out the navy pair, I checked them for mould and found them in perfect order; I pushed my feet into them and quickly gave them a burst of deodorising spray to freshen them up. Moving back down the hallway, I slipped into the bathroom and, checking my reflection in the mirror, grabbed and held the washcloth beneath the cold faucet before dabbing my red, blotchy skin. Ugh, crying so hard never makes for a pretty picture. My eyes were red-rimmed, but I guess if anyone asked, I could pull out the 'just overtired' excuse. "Are you coming?" Garrett yelled down the hallway, and with one more glance, I headed out, catching up with him as he pulled a couple of jackets from the hook and held one up for me to slip my arms into the sleeves. "I think the storms over, but you never know." I nodded, my throat still tight from the personal storm I'd just endured.

The walk to the pub was silent, neither of us willing to break this new truce that sat between us; after all the years of misunderstanding and heartbreak for which we had each wrongly blamed the other, the slate lay clean, waiting for a new chapter to be written. Nothing could ever erase the wasted years; after all, our story had all but ended. Yet, here we were, handed a second chance to write a different ending, maybe right a few wrongs and start something new. We had both changed so much, had suffered from opposing sides; that empty slate was like a bridge over the swirling, writhing river of pain, loneliness and loss, standing firm, just waiting for us to take that first step to cross it, moving forward to the other side.

A bell jingled as we entered the pub, and all heads turned in our direction. "Well, if it isn't little Addison," Jonsie, the barman called out, "long time no see, darlin', what can we be getting for you this fine evening?"

Moving towards the bar as everyone watched, I was hyper-aware of the warm fingers resting along the curve of my spine as Garrett propelled me gently forward. He greeted the crowded tables with a nod here and a murmured "hey" there but never stopped to talk.

"Hi, Jonsie, it's good to see you. I think maybe just a soft drink, um coke with a dash of lime, thanks." I ordered.

His brows rose, "what kind of concoction is that? Coke and lime? Can't say I've heard that one before," he grinned, but he set to, pouring a dash of lime cordial and topping the glass with the fizzy cola and handed it over with a shake of his head. "Whiskey for you, Garrett?"

"Eh, actually, I think I'm all whiskey'd out; I'll have what she's having, live on the wild side." He laughed along with the barman.

"Hey, don't knock it till you tried it," I say, taking a long draw from my straw, "delicious. Are you still cooking up a feast in here, Jonsie? Could do with nice juicy steak n chips, oh, and mushrooms too if you have any."

"Sure thing, little lady. Garrett?"

"Yeah, make it two, but hold the mushrooms." He shuddered at the thought of eating the umbrella-headed fungus and gulped his drink. "Hey, this is surprisingly refreshing; who'd have thought it," he said, frowning at the bubbles in his glass, shook his head and took another sip.

Gathering our glasses, we made our way to one of the booths and had barely sat down when a couple stood and made their way over to us. "Addie, Garrett, we were so sorry to hear about Nate."

"Thank you," I responded, unsure of what else to say. Garrett nodded.

The room erupted with voices, "yeah, sorry for your loss, guys," "my deepest sympathies," "sorry," "cancer, wasn't it?" "he'll be sadly missed," "he was a good Doc," "I'll miss him."

The voices went on, and I just continued to nod, tears welling.

"Right, you lot," Jonsie said as he delivered two plates to the table. "Back off now, let the people eat in peace." He dipped his head in understanding before walking away.

"How did they all find out?"

Garrett shook his head as he wrinkled his nose in thought, "I have no idea. I mean, the first I heard was when I met you on the ferry, and then, of course, I got the telegram when I got home. I know Kemu answered the call from Nate's lawyer, but I don't imagine he would have told anyone in town."

"No, he wouldn't have. Maybe we should ask Jonsie when he comes back over for the plates," I replied, eyeing the veritable feast laid out before us. A large juicy-looking steak took up most of the plate blanketed with golden, thick-cut chips and a generous portion of mushrooms on the side. My mouth watered, my tummy rumbled and using my fingers, I lifted a chip and sank my teeth through the crispy outer layer to find the scorching flesh beneath, hissing through the heat as it burned my fingertips; I thrust the rest of the chip in my mouth and grabbed the knife and fork. I was starving! Not surprising since anything that I'd eaten in the last few days was now feeding the fish after that god-awful ferry crossing. Pushing everything else from my mind, I chomped down the delicious food, barely raising my face until I was mopping the last of the juices from the plate with the few remaining chips.

"Someone was hungry! Good to see you still have a healthy appreciation for food." Garrett's grinning face made me pause for only the slightest of moments before picking the last chip from my plate and rolling it in the mushroom residue, cleaning the plate before popping the now soggy fry into my mouth. Groaning loudly, I sat back and rubbed my belly.

"Oh, my god, that was amazing. Better than I remembered." As I leaned back in my chair, Garrett pushed his plate to the side and hunched forward, elbows on the table.

"Now that I've fed and watered you, would you tell me what you know about Nate's illness?"

I frowned at him, "you make me sound like a horse; you'll be putting me in the stable for the night and rubbing me down ne…." I bit my lip to shut my runaway mouth; that thought should have stayed in my head.

His eyebrows rose, and his lips quirked into a suggestive sneer, "I'm sure I could arrange that."

I blushed furiously, my entire face and neck igniting with embarrassment, or maybe it was just the thought of Garrett's strong hands rubbing along my skin.

"Ugh, hmm," I coughed, clearing my throat and linked my hands in my lap to stop myself from reaching for his. "I told you on the ferry; I wasn't privy to Nate's personal life. Honestly, since walking out of our home over a year ago, I'd not laid eyes on or heard from him at all. When Nate's boss, Randal, the hospital Super', called me that day, I was taken entirely by surprise. It was Randal who told me of Nate's condition and the severity of it. Nate had been diagnosed with pancreatic cancer. I understand it's the most aggressive of cancers and isn't easily detectable; sadly, they caught it too late.

Nate knew his time was short; he asked Randal to call me, insisted that I visit as soon as possible as Nate said it was imperative that we talk. I rushed right over. And as I told you earlier, he gave me a cryptic half message before," I gulped, tears welled, but I blinked them back, "before he was too weak to talk anymore. The doctors came in, and I stood back, waiting for them to do something, anything, but they did nothing, he'd signed a DNR, and they couldn't legally bring him back even when I begged them. I sat with him for the longest time, Garrett. The guilt, the disastrous marriage, the abuse, the regrets all came and went as I sat beside him and held his hand. As much as his cryptic message baffled me, I was happy that he'd reached out, so he didn't have to die alone." I sniffed and took the napkin he was holding out to me.

"I'm glad he wasn't alone as well; thank you for going to see him, especially after the way he treated you."

"All done with the plates?" Jonsie's booming voice came from beside us. "Aww, Addie, girl, has this big eejit been making you cry?" he frowned at Garrett.

I gave him a watery smile and responded, "No, not at all; we were discussing Nate's passing."

"Oh, it's a sad time, lass, c'mere," he said and pulled me from my chair and hugged me in close. "He was a good bloke," he whispered. "A brilliant Doc, and although he never treated you quite right, I know he loved you down deep. He'd speak of you whenever he visited, reminisce a bit, you know, about when you lot were just teens and would try sneaking in here, hoping for a free plate of chips. We'll all miss him," he finished.

"Thank you." I sniffed, pushing away a little and looking up; sad eyes didn't look right on Jonsie, the crinkling of laughter lines proof that this face was typically jovial, always ready for a good chuckle. "Wait, you said when he visited? When did Nate visit?"

"Well, he'd fly that whirlybird of his over every two or three months. He'd land it at the hospital pad and visit with the staff for a bit, talk with the patients in the ward and then come by for a drink or two while he waited for Sonya; she'd drive across with the kids and pick him up. It was sad that you could never make the trip with him, but he explained, you know, about the accident and you not wanting to bring back the sad memories."

"Yes, the memories," I whispered. The little snippets that I'd recalled earlier popping to mind. "Thanks for sharing," I said to Jonsie as I stepped away and watched as he expertly stacked the plates and glasses.

Wait a second! If Garrett had been living on the island the whole time I'd been away, then surely Nate's visits should have given them time to rebuild their relationship? Why hadn't either of them said anything to me? Was I the only one left out? What were they hiding? And who the hell is Sonya, and why was she picking Nate up here, at the pub?

Garrett

Nate was here on the island! He'd been so close; how had he not known? Why hadn't he stayed at the homestead? The only answer to that was Nate hadn't wanted him to know, never intended to bridge the divide that separated them all.

Watching Jonsie clear the table and walk away, he drew his gaze back to Addie; she looked as shell shocked as he felt. His brother had kept secrets from them both. What else had he been hiding? Why had he stayed with the crazy lady rather than here at the pub?

"Whose Sonya?" was the first question Addie asked as she sat back down, her voice barely above a whisper. "Was Nate having an affair with her?"

"I don't know, Addie. I have no idea what their relationship was. I don't know much about Sonya either, for that matter; I do know she has a bunch of kids. She moved into one of the older, empty cottages on the other side of the island; maybe she's a relative of the owners. Can't say I've ever met her; I haven't been on that side of the island for years."

"So, she's not a local then?" she questioned.

I shook my head, "No, not from here originally, but she was here when I came back. I thought maybe you would have known her."

"No, not at all. The name was unfamiliar to me, and the lawyer couldn't elaborate when I asked him about her. If she was on the island before we left ... Oh my god, some of those kids could be his if he had an affair, and that's why he visited all the time. I bet he told her everything, had a jolly good laugh at my expense," her pale face turned red as she got more and more worked up.

"Enough," I barked, "just breath a second. We need proof, don't upset yourself on circumstantial evidence. The only way to get the answers you want is to ask her. We need to track her down and hear what she has to say before you work yourself into a frenzy." I said, reaching for her hand and gently squeezing. She gulped a breath and looked down.

"We?" she asked.

"I don't want you to face her alone, not if she's going to bombard you with information that could potentially hurt. Plus, I was here when you had your accident, and if she mentions that, then I'll be able to tell if she's lying to you. And in all honesty, I need some answers too as to why Nate never came to the homestead."

Addie sat silent, deep in thought.

"Garrett," she said, so quietly I had to lean forward to catch her words. The din from the pub's clientele seemed to ramp up, their volume appearing to push me towards her physically. "Help me remember so that when I face this woman, who seems to be in cahoots with my ex-husband, I can tell for myself whether she is lying."

I studied her face, watching the emotions chase through those gorgeous green eyes. "Ok, baby. Anything for you."

I said, lifting her hand from the table and placing my lips against it. "Just let me go and pay Jonsie, and we can head home."

Placing her hand back down, I walked away, feeling her eyes following me. God help me, I had to find a way to make her remember.

Forcing my way through the crowd near the bar, I settled the bill and turned, only to find myself surrounded by the people I'd ignored for the last three years.

"Good to see you out and about again, Garrett."

"It's been way too long."

"Come visit soon; you've locked yourself away in that house for years."

"Nice to see you, Buddy."

"Don't be a stranger, Garrett. Life's too short, man."

I had no idea people had missed me. I'd been back three years, and this was the first interaction I'd had with the people who had been like family to me growing up. I was overwhelmed with their words, the friendly touches on my arm, and the hugs I received. Feeling guilty and a little over-emotional, I responded with slaps on the back, shaking hands with my old mates as their wives hugged me and promised to visit. With a lump in my throat and eyes burning just a little, I found my way back to the table where Addison sat watching, smiling.

She stood, made her way around the table, and took my arm, walking us both towards the door. Once outside, she released me, and we made our way back up the cobbled pathway. Halfway home, she turned toward me, staying my stride with a hand on my arm.

Shaking her head at me, she spat out, "When you said earlier that you stayed here alone, I had no idea you meant literally."

"Addie, the only person I saw was Kemu. When you and Nate left, someone had to run the business, I suppose if Dad had still been alive, I might have left the island, but, well, there was no one else, and besides, I was in no state to entertain. Even when I went to the city to take the birds in, I'd crate them and take the early ferry, staying with them rather than mingling. I couldn't bear the pity and prying eyes; I had no answers for the questions I knew would be asked. How was I supposed to respond, Addie, when friends undoubtedly would have inquired about you, about Nate? I couldn't listen to their gossip about your lives as husband and wife, your wedding, the pregnancy," I almost whispered the last. "It was all too painful. Living with the knowledge that I'd let you go; all that I'd lost was hard enough, but to have others talk about it, was too much. So, I stayed away." Gripping her hand, I turned and started walking towards home, staring straight ahead so as not to see her reaction, the soft scuffle of her flats and the clunk of my boots on the path, the only sound.

Addison

Curling onto my side, in my skinny bed from yesteryear, I hugged my arms around myself. I'd asked Garrett to help me remember, and I meant it. I needed to know what went down that night. What it was, I'd locked away in my head.

We'd arrived back at the house, the silent walk home should have bothered me, but with his hand holding mine, I found myself strangely content. I was bone-tired; the lack of sleep, the emotional upheaval, the long ferry ride and the food baby I was still cradling set me yawning, barely able to keep my eyes open.

"Bed?" Garrett asked as he assisted me up the stairs and along the hallway.

I nodded, "I'm beat! We'll talk more in the morning, yes?"

"Yeah, sure thing." He pushed open my door and turned quickly, stooping, his lips collided with mine, hard quick, I had little chance to decide how to respond before it was over, and he was walking away. "Oh, and Addie, it's great to have you back," he flung over his shoulder before disappearing into his old room and shutting the door.

His words stayed with me, and my tired brain over-analysed them as I got ready for bed. *'It's great to have you back'* Did that mean back here on the island, back in the homestead, or was there something more, with that brief kiss, was he saying, 'back to him, he had me back?'

I sighed; this wasn't getting me anywhere. Rolling onto my back, I practised the relaxation techniques, learned at my yoga classes, needing my body, as well as my mind to unwind or sleep, would never come. A deep breath in, and I clenched my muscles, counting softly one through ten and then release both muscles and breath, over and over. Heavy limbed, I felt myself begin to melt into the mattress. The distant sound of the ocean lulled my senses, and the only light illuminating the room was from the moon, no light pollution on this tiny piece of paradise. I smiled softly and closed my eyes. I was home.

Bang! The slamming of a door woke me with a jolt. What the hell? What time was it? A glance at my mobile informed me that I'd had my eyes closed longer than the few seconds it felt like and had managed to sleep all night, the grey light of dawn beginning to filter in from behind the curtains, lighting my room little by little. As my eyes leisurely roamed the room, I was surprised to find all my old belongings, nick-nacks collected, once treasured. This room was an excellent place to begin, to re-discover me. To re-live moments in time to attempt to unlock those little doors in my mind.

The crunching of boots on gravel told me Garrett was the reason I was awake this early. I listened to his receding footsteps, knowing he'd be gone for at least a couple of hours checking on any new arrivals, documenting their growth, cleaning and feeding, all those things we used to do together. Now was the perfect opportunity to get reacquainted with the building. Slipping from my warm cocoon of blankets, I snagged the throw from the end of the bed and wrapped it around my shoulders to fight the slight shiver and gooseflesh on my skin, the shorts and tank I'd worn for sleeping in not quite covering enough skin to ward off the morning chill. I was alone in the house, and I snickered at myself when I realized I was tiptoeing, like an imposter, from my room, looking left and right along the hallway and into the spare rooms that had doors standing open. Finally, I stood in the doorway to the main living area, eyes scanning the room. It looked tired, rundown, not grubby; no, Kemu would never have that. All was tidy, nothing out of place. But the closer I looked, the more I realized the whole area needed a good lick of paint. A touch of colour would add new life, refresh the old place. The décor was probably the same from when Garretts Mum had left, all those years ago. Should I dare suggest a change? And then it dawned on me; I now owned half of this property. What had been Nate's was now mine.

Poor Nate, this place must have held some sad memories for him not to return on his visits. Or maybe, it was because Garrett had been living here; it made me wonder what their fight had been over. Whatever it was, it must have been something pretty damn serious to split the brothers apart to the extent that neither of them was willing to breach the gaping chasm in their relationship. Without really thinking about it, I'd moved back down the hall and stopped before a closed door, hand on the knob. Taking a deep breath, I turned it and pushed the door wide. Still not ready to take the step across the threshold, I took in the room before me, eyes drawn to the far corner where, once upon a time, the space had been occupied by a bassinet piled high with tiny outfits, books and teddys', waiting, for a child that never got to lay within it. The corner stood empty now, all traces of our child gone.

Nate had turned away as he confessed that there was nothing left. I'd asked him to bring me a cuddly toy, something which belonged to our baby, to hold as I mourned. He'd broken the news that in his fury, devastated over the loss of his child and the shock of nearly losing his wife; he'd gone a little crazy, breaking and burning reminders of what was lost. He'd left me nothing to hold. The only proof my pregnancy actual happened was the red scar across my bikini line.

As I looked around the room now, it was difficult to imagine his breakdown. The king-sized bed looked inviting with a throw blanket and piles of pillows; a matching towel, hand towel and flannel set placed on the edge of the mattress; the bedside table housed a jar. What was that? I strode into the room and picked up the glass jar filled with candle wax, tipping it to the side to read the label. Lavender, it was my favourite, and Kemu, bless his soul, had remembered that. I guess he'd left it as a welcome home gift, and I had been so bull-headed, wanting my old room without pausing to think he may have done something so sweet.

Sinking to the edge of the bed, I dragged open the drawers in the nightstand, searching for a booklet of matches or a lighter, rummaging through odd nuts and bolts, toothpicks, old receipts, ripped, empty, silver-foil condom envelopes, jeez how many had we used? It was like a rubbish bin in here! A flashlight, fridge magnets, and beneath all the flotsam and jetsam, wedged between the back of the drawer and Nate's heavy medical encyclopaedia was a cigarette lighter. Aha, Jackpot. The little wheel whirred beneath my thumb once, twice, and I was rewarded with fire the third time. Holding the candle at an angle, I touched the flame to the wick. It hissed a little, like a cornered cat, as the heat seared the excess wax, but finally, it caught, and I set the candle back down. Throwing the lighter back in the drawer, my hand hovered over the sizeable medical volume. It had been Nate's pride and joy, and when not being read, had its very own stand on the shelf so it could be displayed for everyone to see. Why would it be hidden in the bottom of the drawer? As I raised the cover, the nick-nacks resting on it slid to the side and grasping the spine, I heaved the book free. A piece of paper caught my eye, maybe Nate's bookmark or a reminder note. Tugging free the marker, I read the notation on the top corner, *summer 2011.* Turning it over, I was shocked when I came face to face with a much younger me.

I studied my seventeen-year-old self; I had been so skinny. Sharp angled hip bones almost cut through the tiny bikini briefs, and minuscule triangles covered my hardly-there boobs. The faded photo couldn't hide the green in my eyes, which stared just beyond the camera, and a smile lit my face; but the hair, oh my god, I'd forgotten those blue tips, I'd dyed them over and over before they finally took in my red hair, it seemed like a million years ago.

Popping the photograph in the waistband of my shorts, since I didn't have a pocket so that I could show Garrett later, I gathered up the volume and moved to the shelf and located the book stand built specifically for it. More papers slipped down and poked out from between the pages as I stood the heavy volume on its end. Frowning, I wondered out loud, "what else has he hidden away in his medical bible?" Snatching it back up, I paced back to the bed and began turning the pages.

I found photo after photo, haphazardly spaced throughout the encyclopaedia, it seemed Nate had used his most precious belonging as a photo album dedicated to me. Every picture I plucked from between the pages were dated by season and year, documenting my life on the island. Happiness and innocence radiated brightly from each of the prints, and I smiled, lifting them from the book and making a pile on the bedspread. I noted that I was smiling or laughing in every shot, oblivious to the camera and that I was being immortalized on film, never once looking directly into the lens. The outfits made me chuckle; the old dresses I wore, corduroy pants and ruffled tops, outrageous, I would be shuddering if it wasn't so funny. I turned to the next page, and my smile faltered as I took in the torn look on my face. I knew without checking the rear precisely when Nate had taken this photo. The day Garrett broke my heart and stole my happiness away. The look of desolation in my tear-filled eyes. The laughing girl-child from the picture before, forever lost.

I lowered it slowly, adding it to the growing pile and wondered why Nate had kept such an appalling photo, and then I turned the page, and there was another one and another. All were featuring sad, glassy eyes screaming heartache and loneliness. What the hell, Nate, why would he have taken these, let alone kept them. How many more had he hidden away? Tipping the book on its end, I watched in disbelief as another dozen or so pictures floated free. Once they'd settled on the bed, the book bounced as I threw it onto the pillow and stared at the portraits of me, my hand going to my mouth as a gasp escaped. The one laying nearest portrayed me standing in my bedroom wearing the white, flowing sundress I was married in, a sprig of heather in one hand and a photograph of Garrett in the other; my eyes scrunched closed as hot tears flowed down pale cheeks. Studying the photo, I worked out the cameraman had been outside of my window. If Nate was close enough to capture this memory, then he had to have seen why I was so upset;

he'd probably watched as I'd slowly taken down the more intimate pictures of Garrett and myself. Hell, I could still remember the pain I felt that morning, as I'd kissed the black and white images before securing them away in the back of a drawer. Broken-hearted as I said Goodbye to Garrett, and Nate had captured the moment.

I cast my gaze to the next photo; breath hitched in my throat, and tears weld as I reached for it, holding it close to my chest as I moved to turn the remaining pictures over and then, I broke. The damn erupted, and I screamed out my grief; as my tears fell, and I slid from the bed to the floor. The pictures, like confetti, floated and settled around me as I sat sobbing.

That was where Garrett found me, sitting amongst the snapshots of my life, one clutched in my fingers, showing my abdomen swollen with child, my hands gently cradling the life within me.

Garrett

My early morning sojourn to see the newborns was usually the highlight of my day-to-day dealings at the sanctuary, but today, my thoughts weren't on the chicks we were rearing. No, my thoughts lay with the red-haired woman at the house. We'd made in-roads into fixing our shattered relationship last night, and I had barely pulled myself away once arriving home from town. The brief kiss, my lips touching hers, shit, I deserved a medal for not picking her up and throwing her on the bed. My body craved hers, my soul starved for the love we once shared.

Placing the last chick back in the breeding box, I decided I couldn't go another moment without being in the same space as Addie and withdrew from the room, the chirping birds going silent as I left. Closing the door carefully behind me, I turned and legged it back to the main house heading straight for her room, just a peak; it was all I needed, for now, to know she was sleeping soundly, tucked up and dreaming, hopefully of me.

Opening the door just a crack, I peered in and then thrust the door wide. An empty room greeted me. Where could she be? Heading down the hall, I poked my head into my room, nothing, and continued until I stopped outside Nate's bedroom door and heard the stifled sobs coming from within.

Shit! Had I misread all the signs? Was Addie missing Nate? He had been her husband, after all. Should I knock and go in? Or should I walk away and leave her to her grieving? So many questions to which I had no answers.

A hiccupping breath, followed by another onslaught of tears, she needed to be held. Decision made, I entered the room to find Addie slumped in a messy puddle on the floor, dressed in the tiniest little tank top and short shorts, which I couldn't help but notice, showed a deliciously rounded arse, as she huddled in the foetal position. Strewn on the floor surrounding her were several photographs.

"Addie, baby. C'mere," I whispered, dropping to the floor, with my back resting against the bed. I gently drew her up and into my arms. Her sobbing continued while I cradled her chilled body; noting the goosebumps on her skin, I grabbed the throw from where it lay discarded on the floor beside us and wrapped it around her quivering body. Rocking gently, I murmured into her hair. "It's ok, Addie. Let it all out, baby. I know it's a shock being back here, bringing all the feelings back. Grief does that, sneaks up when you least expect it." The sobs turned to sniffles as I talked. "Shh now, come on, that's it. It's normal to miss him; he wa…."

"Miss him!" she reared back, her eyes furious, "Miss him, I hate him. He was a lying asshole, a bully and a freaking stalker to boot."

My god, she was beautiful, even with the red nose and puffy eyes. She shifted in my lap, the throw dropping to the floor, and my hands lowered to my sides. All I wanted to do was kiss her, kiss away every hurt, every sad memory, push her back to the mat and cover that lush body with my own. And then her words penetrated my sex-starved mind.

"Huh? You hate him? Then why are you crying?" What had I missed here?

Addie took a breath, and in a voice, raspy from crying, answered my query. "After my accident, I pleaded with Nate, begged him to bring me something belonging to our baby; a toy, a book, anything. And he denied me.

Later, he told me he'd been grief-stricken and couldn't handle memories of the pregnancy and our little lost soul, that he'd come home that night and stripped the room of reminders, burning it all. And I believed him, forgave him. The lying bastard, he still had this!"

She turned the photo so I could see, and my breath caught in my throat as I stared at the snapshot of Addison, her eyes wide with wonder as her hands held her extremely pregnant belly. I felt the blood leave my face; the last time I saw it, that dress was ripped, dusty, and covered in blood. Hell, the photograph could have been taken on that fateful day, mere moments before I walked into that room and changed everything.

Swallowing hard, I pushed the nightmare image away and took a deep breath. "Addie, I'm so sorry he did this to you, but on the bright side, you now have what you craved. You have something more special than a toy you'd chosen or a garment that never got worn. You have visual proof your baby existed. You have a photograph! I turned the image to face her once more, "Just look at how beautiful you are," I whispered as I thumbed away the tears on her cheeks. Dragging her body forward, I wrapped my arms tightly around Addie, her face nestled in the crook of my neck, her free arm slipping around my waist.

Time stood still, it could have been seconds, minutes, or hours that I held her, but I knew it would never be long enough. My arse had gone numb from the hardwood floor, and pins and needles were partying in my feet, yet I was reluctant to move, to break the moment. Finally, squirming a little to get the blood flowing, I released one arm from around her and, grasping the bed frame, hauled our entwined bodies off the floor to the bed, and still, she didn't move.

But a whisper floated past my ear, too quiet for me to catch. "Sorry, Sweetheart, I missed that, say again?"

"I shouldn't have married him." She repeated. "I didn't love him, but I didn't want to hurt him either. I couldn't bring myself to tell him that I was still in love with someone else. But he did know, didn't he? He knew the whole time! Every photo he took of me, there isn't one of them that had me looking into the lens, looking at him. My smile was always for the person behind him, always aimed at you, Garrett. And when we were no longer together, Nate continued to photograph me, capturing my sorrow, the sadness I wore like clothing. He knew it all, and yet he still married me. Why? Why would he marry someone who clearly wanted someone else?"

"Nate was infatuated with you because I loved you. I have no doubt he grew to love you too. The very first time we all met, Nate and I were in a playoff on the basketball court; all our lives, it seems we were competing for something, whether it be who would eventually run the business here, to which of us had Dad's affection, always a contest. When I couldn't take my eyes off you as you walked away, Nate noticed my interest in you, and it was game on. The three of us were inseparable, and even though we had eyes for each other, he never gave up hope that he'd somehow win the girl. And he did win; in his mind, he won the prize because of my selfish stupidity. He waited in the sidelines, biding his time until I fucked up, and he swooped in."

She raised her head, eyes sad as they sought mine. "Garrett, I wasn't a prize, something to be played for in a tug of war. I'm a person who got badly hurt in the games he played. I don't know whether to be furious at you both or sympathise for having to feel the need to compete for everything. Yes, you had the "prize"," she air quoted with her fingers, "and then made the decision to give it away. Who can blame Nate for snatching it up? And then he took it to the next level; he married and created a child. Look where that got us; we all lost. We are broken and alone. You live here running the business and hiding from life, Nate lived with a wife he abused and died lonely, and I live my life trying desperately to remember, to get back my missing memories. I don't think the competition was worth all this heartache." She climbed from my lap, and I watched as she began collecting the photographs. She placed the pile on the bedside table, propping the one of her holding her unborn child against the stack, then bent to blow out the flickering flame in the jar.

I stood and took her face in my hands, forcing her gaze to meet my own. "I've never seen you as a prize, Sweetheart. More like a gift, you gave your heart to me once, but I was young, and I was stupid, not realizing what a precious gem you'd given me. I'm not young now, and I'm certainly not stupid enough to ever give you up again if you give me another chance. I love you, Addie. I always have; that's why I came back. I should never have caught that early ferry back to the city that morning; if only I'd stayed and you'd woken to my face and not Nate's, life would have been so different. But we can't live on 'what ifs'; we can't change the past. I guess what I'm asking is, 'are you willing to give us another try? Give me another try?"

Her eyes flickered back and forth, judging, considering, easily reading the emotions in my own, and slowly she leant in, closing the distance, and her lips touched mine. It could have been a kiss goodbye, but that wasn't what I was after, so instead, I took it as a resounding 'yes' and crushed her to me. My body burned as her touch danced across my abs, her fingers making quick work on the buttons as I shimmied her tank down her arms, pulling her hands free of the material, until finally, we were skin to skin, her soft breasts felt heavenly against my heaving chest.

It had been far too long since she'd been in my arms like this, and there was no chance of going slow. Hands, lips, touching everywhere as if we were on a deadline, and we had to get our fill before our time was up, the need so great, to reacquaint our bodies. Wrapping my leg around hers, I put her off balance, and as I released her, she toppled backwards onto the bed, her hands still reaching. I took two seconds to drink her in before seizing her tiny, short-shorts and dragged them down those beautiful legs before shucking my jeans and shirt and joining her on the covers.

Soft lips kissed, sharp teeth nipped, and her sensual tongue stroked against my own, and when her hand snuck between us and grasped my hard length, I knew that going slow was impossible. Gently disengaging her fingers, I whispered into her mouth. "Baby, if you touch me, I'm not gonna last."

Pulling back slightly, she grinned up at me, "Well then, I guess second time round will have to be the slow one. I want you, Garrett; it's been far too long," she said, arching her back to grind against me. I leant across to the nightstand and dragged open the drawer, fingers searching and finding a foil wrapper, empty, so was the next and the next, I threw them on the floor exasperated, what the hell Nate.

"Garrett," she whispered as I continued my search, "baby, you don't need one." My fingers stopped walking, and I turned a querying frown her way. "It's safe; you won't get me pregnant."

"If you're sure?" she nodded. My cock ached with the idea of going bareback; we'd only ever done that once before and that… I shoved the memory aside and slipped between her legs, gripping my shaft; I stroked my head through her eagerness, slicked, primed, I pushed forward, her hips rose to greet me, as she welcomed me back home.

Addison

It had been so long! Garrett was the only man to have ever touched me this way.

Nate and I had a sex life but never a love life. We fucked like bunnies during ovulation. Yes, Nate was all about impregnating me as soon as possible after I'd recovered from my accident. But each month, my period arrived, and with it, Nate's anger increased, along with the mounting abuse he flung at me, both verbally and physically. His screaming, scathing comments about my looks, size, ability to please a man, as his hands slapped at me, fists flying, and then finally, one day his fury took over completely, and he unknowingly spat the very words that would give me my freedom. "I could fuck you every day, and you'd never give me a child, you infertile bitch." He'd slapped a hand across his mouth as soon as the words came out, and I crawled out from beneath him for the very last time. I had speculated whether my fall had left any physical long-term side effects, and Nate just confirmed those fears; he would know, after all, he wasn't just my husband, but also a brilliant doctor. I finally had my answer.

I built my relationship with Nate on the shame of wanting his brother and the guilt of losing his child, not on love. Discovering that Nate knowingly allowed me to hope for another child month after month was like a knife to my heart: he must hate me! He'd watched my pain every time my period came and then tortured me with unkind words, making me believe I was worthless. But, with Nate's angry outburst, I was done! Infertility set me free of my sham of a marriage.

That intense feeling as countless nerve endings in my lady parts tingled. It had been forever since I'd felt like this. Garrett was the only one that seemed to have the ability to make my skin pebble as if cold at his touch whilst an infernal heat scorched my insides. It was too much, the ache, the wanting, the needing, intensified, and I had to have him right now.

Sadness surged through my mind as Garrett fumbled for a condom he wouldn't need. But the look in his eyes, the intense hunger, chased away all thought and relit my flame. Garrett pushed forward, and my body arched to greet him, stretching miraculously as he fully seated himself inside of me. Withdrawing only slightly, he drove deep again, over and over. We moved together, each thrust propelling us higher, reaching for our release. The friction of his body brushing against my tingling bundle of nerves, so intense I screamed his name as my body spasmed and my orgasm erupted, muscles contracting, gripping him so tight. He continued to thrust as I rode out my release; his panting breath beside my ear told me how close he was, and the deep groan as he fought to hold on, not yet willing to finish, had my body clenching again. Lifting my legs, I wrapped them around his back, crossing my ankles and pinning my heels to his arse, I felt him sink deeper, triggering another orgasm as his cock pulsed, and he cried out my name as we climaxed together.

My breathing was heavy as my legs released their hold, and I fell back against the blankets as I tenderly kissed his chin, his lips, his cheeks, wherever I could reach; my lips touched, familiarizing myself once again with the only man I'd ever truly loved.

Taking me with him, he rolled us till I was on top, still connected as he gripped the blankets on both sides and tugged them up, bringing them together at my back, like a door closing us in a tiny, confined space of a closet.

"Give me a minute or two, Sweetheart, and we'll go again. I wasn't joking about going for seconds, and I'm already feeling the need arising to go for round two if you're up for it?"

I squirmed against him and clenched my inner muscles, which elicited a moan.

"Oh, God, a simple 'yes' would have done fine, but oh-h…" he stopped as I gripped him again, and again all the time feeling him grow, expanding, hardening inside me, and I grinned down at him as his eyes flickered and his breath caught.

Totally in control, I began to rock gently at first, watching my man as I moved. Each movement forward put pressure on my pleasure point, and I started to grind, and it still wasn't enough. I sat up. The chill air between us had my nipples pebbling, and I instantly missed the feel of his warm skin against mine. But the feeling of his erection pressed deep inside me overrode any other thought. My body took control, and I began to ride Garrett's body like a rodeo queen, the blankets flapping like wings as I moved. His hips bucked beneath my arse as if to unseat me as we moved together until a harsh cry flew from my lips, and a growl erupted from Garrett as he drove deep, triggering our release. His head dropped back to the pillow as if drugged, his eyes semi-closed and a smile tugging at his lips. "Oh, my, god", he whispered, "I've missed you."

"I missed you too," I said, dropping my body to lie against his. "So much so that I could lay here all day except…."

"Except what, Babes?" he asked, worry furrowing his brow.

"Except," I grinned. "I want coffee, no, I need coffee."

"Right then, quick shower?" he wriggled his brows, and I chuckled.

"Not again, I think three times in half an hour might be pushing it," I laughed at him, and he silenced me with his lips on mine, a punishing kiss which left me breathless. Now it was his turn to laugh as he released me, and I came up gasping for air.

"Come on," pushing me to the side, he heaved himself off the bed and then held out his hand and hauled me up to his side. Oops, upright, I felt the tell-tale sign of *what goes up, must come down* and, slamming my thighs together, proceeded to penguin walk behind Garrett into the ensuite. Moving as quickly as possible behind the ceramic screen to use the toilet whilst he opened the shower stall and fiddled with the taps. Garrett climbed into the shower humming softly to himself. Smiling to myself, I thought I could quickly become accustomed to making love with my man and sharing a bathroom every morning.

As I finished cleaning up and flushed the loo, a loud "FUCK" came from the direction of the shower, and I watched as Garrett jumped out of the waters flow.

"Sorry," I screeched. "I forgot flushing affects the temperature in there."

Pulling a face, I slid the door open, trying not to giggle at the shocked look on his face. "Um, are you ok?" I asked as an arm shot forward and dragged me into the stream of cold water. I shrieked and tried to escape, but he wrapped me in his arms and held me in place till the water ran warm, laughing at me as I wriggled and screamed.

Pinning me in place, he kissed me soundly, the intensity of his lips taking away my breath as I melted against his body. Drifting, carried away on the tide of feelings, re-awakened. His kisses were hard and passionate one moment, then softly nibbling, nipping at my lips the next, and my response was needy, greedy as I moaned softly, his mouth closed over mine, swallowing my sounds. His skin slick beneath my roving hands, and as I came up for air, my lips followed their path as they shimmied across his shoulders and chest, my greedy tongue seeking the droplets of water beading his body and I felt him begin to rise against my hip and hastily pushed away. "Uh, no!

Down boy," I chuckled, "this girl wants her coffee, a promise is a promise, Mr." Taking up the loofah, I quickly soaped him up. Then taking hold of the shower nozzle, I rinsed the suds from his back, then reached around, and wrapping my hand around his now hardened appendage, manoeuvred him in the direction of the door before releasing him. "Be a love and put the kettle on, would you? I'll be out in a minute."

"Huh, what?" he spluttered, looking down in dismay to where my hand had just been. "I could stay, wash your back for you." He said, hopefully, turning back toward me with a grin and a wink.

"Out, now!" I pulled the shower door closed and turned my back on temptation. I smiled, listening to him growl something about 'coffee being a cock-block' as he grabbed a towel and headed out of the bathroom.

After adding more soap to the loofah and lathering my skin, my nipples tingled, still hyper-sensitive from his attentions on them early. In my nether regions, the satisfying ache I hadn't felt in years bought to mind that fateful morning when I'd sat on the loo and realized I'd had sex with Nate whilst dreaming of Garrett. The wonderful dream that I now knew hadn't been a dream at all. Did that mean I hadn't had sex with Nate? Had he simply slipped between the sheets, needing to be close after he'd lost his patient and held me while I slept? Turning the shower off, I tucked myself into a large fluffy towel and walked back to the bedroom.

The dishevelled bed, blankets in disarray bore evidence of our lovemaking, and I quickly pulled the covers straight, just in case Kemu happened by, then bent to pick up the discarded foil wrappers that Garrett had dropped on the floor. I stilled with one in my hand and then reached for another; realization struck; Nate always used a condom, right up until we discovered I was pregnant. I recalled the moment I'd come back from the bathroom carrying the positive pregnancy stick.

"Nate, it's a double blue line. I'm pregnant." Nate had been resting against the pillows, arms folded behind his head. Now he sat forward, his hand held out.

"Let me see." He demanded, and I held the stick out for him to take.

He stared for long moments at the offending blues and then shrugged. "I guess the plan for a family, in a year, has been blown out of the water, babe. Please remind me to tell my patients that condoms are most definitely not 100% effective. We're having a baby, Addison. I'm so happy, honey, how are you feeling? We'll have to get you to the office for a check-up, pre-natal vitamins and bloods."

I shook my head, still in shock. "I, I err." I blew out a breath and tried again. "I'm a little overwhelmed; we've been so careful." I gave the top drawer, which held the condoms, a scathing glare. I smiled tentatively at Nate, "If you're happy, then so am I." I proclaimed. "It's just a shock, I mean, we've barely had time to get used to married life, six weeks is no time at all, and now there's going to be a baby.

A honeymoon child!" I shook my head as I took back the stick and retreated to the bathroom, threaded it back into the wrapper, disposed of it in the bin below the vanity, and then stared at myself in the mirror. 'Oh, God. A baby! Well, that was unexpected.

Now, staring at the wrappers in my hand, my breath left me as if someone sucker-punched me. "No," I whimpered. "Oh, God, No." I'd had my pregnancy examination, which had shown I was six weeks pregnant. Six weeks married, six weeks pregnant, that meant I'd fallen the first time we'd had sex. And as Nate never had sex without a condom, the timing fit, the engagement party, the sexy dream that I now knew wasn't a dream!

My legs gave way, and I collapsed into a heap on the floor, staring wide-eyed as tears gathered, overflowed, and dripped to the carpet. A sob tore from my throat, and I clenched my fist against my chest to ease the shooting pain as the realization struck hard and fast. The baby I lost wasn't Nate's at all; it was Garretts!

Garrett

This stupid grin just wouldn't leave my face. As I rushed around the kitchen, pouring beans into the coffee maker and flicking the switch before, almost dancing across the room, my body and mind were lighter than they'd been in years. I placed the cups on the silver tray and waited for the water to heat, catching a glimpse of my upturned lips reflected in the polished machine, and I chuckled, what kind of witchery did that woman possess? She'd turned my world right-side-up again in a mere twenty-four hours. Life was no longer just bearable. I was flying high, on love, on life; that was the magic Addison brought into my life. I wasn't going to fuck this up, not everyone got a second chance to make things right, and I damned well meant to grasp our burgeoning relationship in an iron-clad hold, solid, unbreakable.

We could start fresh, forget the pain of loss, the ugliness of arguments and petty jealousies.

Addison was still a no-show as the slow drip, drip of coffee finally stopped, and I doctored both drinks, hoping she hadn't altered how she took her coffee. I wondered if she'd snook back into bed after her shower. I was up for that! Snagging both cups in one hand and the biscuit tin with the other, I retraced my steps back to the master bedroom and came to a stand-still, coffee sloshing over the rim, splattering against the skirting. Addison was sitting where I'd initially found her, a crying, heaving mess on the floor. Shit, was she regretting what just happened?   It seemed I might have been a little presumptuous about starting a new life together.

Striding into the room and throwing the tin on the bed, I carefully stepped past her and put the cups on the dresser, squatting to her level, I gently palmed her chin, forcing her to look at me, her eyes, red, brimming with tears, the look almost brought me to my knees. So much hurt, so much regret. Releasing her face, I grasped her clenched fists and slowly peeled her fingers back to reveal the foil wrappers. My brows furrowed as my brain attempted to piece together what had happened here. Taking the rubbish from her and placing it beside the cooling coffee, I turned back to find her studying me like she was waiting for something, a reaction, a word, I just didn't know.

Sniffling and hiccupping, the quiet sobs, a breathy hitch in her throat, her cheeks wet from the river of tears she'd wept, hair still damp from the shower stuck to her skin, hiding parts of her face from me. I moved, meaning only to push the hair back, needing to see all of her as I tried to guess what had caused this latest breakdown, but as I lifted my hand, she flinched, cowering, and it almost broke my heart. Was this fear-filled reaction something my brother had instilled? How often had he struck out at her? Moving more slowly, my palm open, fingers gentle on her face as I moved the strands of hair, smoothing them behind her ears before cupping her face, thumbs carefully caressing her cheekbones as I swiped away her tears.

"Talk to me, baby. I need to understand," I whispered. And Addison reacted.

I found myself toppling backwards, my body smashing against the cabinet, coffee slopping over the rims of the cups like a tidal wave, my arse hit the ground, my arms folding around the naked, shaking body that had launched itself into my lap.

"T-t-two y-y-years w-w-wasted," she stuttered out between sobs.

Ah, now I understood. Addison was resentful of the time we'd missed out on being together. Damn that early morning ferry ride. If only we had called each other, but I'd promise her I'd give her time to break things with Nate without my interference. Phew, I'd thought for a minute she was regretting the magic we'd shared earlier.

"Hush now," I crooned as I gently rocked her back and forth, "our time apart gave us time to grow; if I'd not lost you, I'd never have known this feeling of contentment, holding you, loving you again."

She pushed back against my hands, and I released my grip on her as she leant back to look at my face.

"N-no, you don't understand," she sniffed, trying desperately to stifle the sobs causing her to stutter, dashing the tears from her eyes with her fists. She swallowed hard, and I wondered what disaster she was about to unleash. "I st-stayed with Nate for t-two years because of the guilt I felt losing his child. But Nate always used a condom." She fell silent, waiting, watching me intently. What was I meant to say? Why was she telling me this? And then it clicked. Addison had figured out that the baby may have been mine.

Shit, shit, shit. I'd know that Addison recalling her hidden memories would reveal our fight and what it was about on the night of her accident. I was ready to answer all those questions, but Addie hadn't recovered the memory from that night; no, she'd come to this conclusion from a different direction entirely. I was unsure now what to reveal and what to keep secret. Caught up in my internal battle of what I could or couldn't say, I didn't realize my silence spoke for me as she scrutinized my face and drew back further, "you knew!" she accused.

I brought my hands to my face, rubbing my cheeks, knuckling my eyes as if that could remove the truth from showing, biding time, deciding what to say. Dropping my arms, I let my eyes meet hers, responding quietly.

"I suspected that the baby could have been mine, yes."

Her eyes widened, "Oh god!" she whispered, sliding from my body and climbing warily to her feet. She picked up her towel and wrapped it around her as she moved out into the hall, her bare feet shuffling across the wooden floors, with me trailing behind her into the living room where she suddenly stopped, turned and with a shattered look on her face, repeated my words.

"The baby could be mine!"

In this room, on this exact damn spot, I had confronted her. And now she remembered.

Addison

"I remember!" my anguished voice held so much pain as visions of that fateful night played like a movie in my mind.

The storm raged. The window shutter in the office had been banging intermittently for the last two hours, but no way in hell was I going out in this weather to fasten it down again. It must have blown free after Nate left in the early hours of the morning, responding to whatever emergency haled him.

"Kemu, is that you?" I called as the screen door creaked open and then slammed closed as the ferocious winds caught it. The rain had finally slowed from its monsoon-like rage, but the sky still threatened, clouds hung heavy with rain yet to come. The soft fall was a mere sprinkling to what had been, but still enough to soak to the skin. The shredded leaves and dust turned to red mud, creating a slippery hazard on the pathways, and Nate had warned me not to leave the house.

"Kemu?" I called again and heaved my heavily pregnant body from the sofa. I really must start sitting in the armchair; it would make standing up so much easier. I turned toward the door and froze on the spot, shock written across my face as I stared across the expanse of the living room at a dripping Garrett.

He, like me, stood unmoving in the doorway. The surprise on his face, as his eyes took me in, quickly morphed to something much darker. I could feel the anger radiating from him, a storm indoors was imminent, and I had no idea why.

As he took a menacing step toward me, I noticed the puddle he'd left in the doorway and the watery trail which followed him until he stopped a mere metre from me.

"G-Garrett," I stuttered. "How, how are you here? The ferry surely was cancelled."

His eyes that, until now, hadn't left my rounded belly rose slowly up my torso, passed my breasts and climbed the column of my neck; finally reaching my face, his eyes claimed mine, and a shudder ran through me. I'd never experienced the force of Garrett's anger, and the fiery heat in his gaze nearly burned me alive.

Lost in his molten eyes, I didn't see his hand whip forward, and I jumped as his fingers gripped my hand and raised it between us.

"What the fuck is this?" he spat. My eyes shifted to where he was looking. My wedding band cut slightly into my flesh, where my finger had swollen with the weight I'd gained during my pregnancy.

I was second-guessing the whole secret marriage thing now that the man I'd loved my entire life was standing in front of me. We should have told him. I, I should have told him. The heated room caused steam to rise from his wet clothing, adding fuel to the image of the burning rage inside of him. I snatched my hand away.

"He, um, I mean we, Nate and me, we decided life was too short to wait… we, um, we got married."

"When?" he growled. "Before or after he knocked you up?"

"It, it wasn't like that." My lips were so dry, my tongue darted out, and his gaze followed the action. My heartbeat was hard and fast as I watched the flame in his eyes change from anger to need and back again in an instant. I swallowed and continued, "J-Jimmy died, the night of our engagement party and Nate," I paused as his face grew dark with the mention of his brother's name, "and Nate was so distraught when he got back from the hospital. I, we, I mean, that was when we decided to, j-just go ahead, why wait?"

"Why wait?" he echoed, his voice dangerous, low.

He was scaring me. I'd fought with Garrett many times over the years when angered, he'd yell back, but I was never frightened of his loud, overbearing voice, this though, this was different; He didn't raise his voice now, his tone a controlled growl which I felt like a bass vibration rumbling through me. I'd seen him angry, but I'd never seen him furious. The question was, why? Why was he like this? What had I done? I puffed myself up, hid my fear behind my confusion.

"What the hell was I meant to be waiting for? You made it pretty clear you didn't give two hoots about our engagement; we invited you to celebrate with us. But no, you decided to play the spoilt-brat and chose not to make an appearance." The dream flew to my mind, and I hastily pushed it back into its box and locked it down. "And now you have the audacity to walk in here eight months later and play the injured party? Well, fuck you, Garrett."

He took a step closer, his body almost touching my bulging waistline, and I couldn't suppress the quiver of fear that rolled down my spine. Where the hell was Kemu?

Garrett's voice dropped even lower as he growled deep in his throat. "I've worked my arse off for the last eight months! I finished the course in half the time, scrimped and saved, cut all ties to my friends, and searched out the best Manager I could to take over my position. As promised!" He gripped my upper arms and gave me a slight shake. "The whole time, I knew you'd be waiting. I knew you'd have a hard time breaking up with Nate, but I never once thought you'd stab me in the back and marry the bastard."

"Stab you in the back? You're talking in riddles, Garrett. You left me, broke my heart, and now you're back getting all heavy-handed, and I haven't a clue why? You didn't want me, but you don't want Nate to have me either?"

The emotions flitting across his face, anger, regret and was that confusion?

"You promised me!" he whispered is voice breaking. "Promised you'd wait for me. And you married him anyway." He shook his head and stepped away.

"Wait, what? When?"

He huffed out a hurt chuckle. "When you ask? You played me, and I fell for it. I thought our night together was a fresh start, our second chance. Was it payback? I broke your heart, so you broke mine?" The hurt, the anger in his voice was as painful to listen to as the words themselves.

"Garrett, you're not making any sense. When did I promise you?"

He whipped to face me once more. "The same night, everyone else celebrated your upcoming nuptials. Your damned engagement party, of course. What, are you telling me I was that forgettable? Way to make a guy feel special, Addison."

I recalled the day in question, the hopes I'd had as I'd stood at the docks waiting for someone who never showed. My hand rose to touch my cheek, where I could still feel the ghostly sting of Nate's slap, a reminder of my stupidity. The people milling around the house and the garden, smiling, drinking, eating until the call came in from the hospital, and they all cleared out, and I was left alone, Cinderella, left behind to clean up the mess. I rebelled, leaving the half-eaten plates of food, the dirty glasses exactly where they were, and climbed instead into a tequila bottle. I'd dreamt of Garrett that night, but there was no way I would tell him that.

"You were always special to me, Garrett. I waited for you to step off the ferry; for hours, I waited. You didn't come."

"I came in time to pull you out of a tequila bottle," he retorted, and I gasped.

"You, you came. You were here that night?"

He looked at me like I was some kind of lunatic.

"Damn straight. I was here. I made coffee, tried to sober you up. We talked. Made promises to each other. We made love," he gave a derogative snort, "or maybe I made love, and you had sex," he snarled. "Because it obviously didn't mean anything to you. You up and married my brother anyway."

I couldn't look at him. If what he said was true, then I hadn't been dreaming. He and I, it had all happened. Another thought struck me like a hammer blow; the night in question was when I conceived my baby. Did that mean?

Breathing suddenly seemed the most challenging thing to do. I couldn't remember how. Like a goldfish, my mouth opened and closed, trying to remember how to inhale as a full-blown panic attack struck. With the lack of oxygen, my head spun, and I collapsed in a heap on the floor. For long moments I floundered, gasping, drawing breath, hissing it out, in, out faster and faster. My head continues to spin; the baby, most likely feeling the effects of my attack, began kicking painfully up beneath my ribs. I was going to be sick. Make it stop, make it stop. My eyes flickered wildly, light to dark and light again as they rolled back and then a hand to the back of my head, steadying, calming as a brown paper bag appeared before me. I grabbed the lifeline in both my hands breathing fast, ballooning the bag with my breath, and then sucking back in; the lingering smell of the take-

out meal ghosted the tastebuds on my tongue, as I finally found control, slow and deep, inhale, exhale.

"Thank you," I closed my eyes and allowed myself a moment of peace. And then the baby kicked again, and a crippling pain almost retook my breath; I couldn't stop the grimace or the gasp, and Garrett's all-seeing eyes narrowed.

"How far along are you?" he asked. His warm hand disappeared from my head, and he stepped away.

"Eight months," I whispered and glanced up at him, watching the cogs click into place.

"That means the baby could be mine!"

Coming back to the present, I found Garrett's eyes fixed on my face, watching, waiting as my memories clicked into place.

"I'm so sorry, Garrett," I whispered, "I didn't know. If only I could have remembered earlier, you wouldn't have suffered the loss alone. I don't understand why Nate would blame you for my accident unless - did Nate know?" I had to ask.

"Yes!" he croaked, then cleared his throat. "That was the reason we fought and never spoke again. I was here waiting; it seemed like forever that I sat, in the dark, nursing that bottle of whiskey, all the time praying you'd make it through the surgery, and then he came in the door. Thanks to the booze, I was a little slow off the mark, but Nate's fist slamming into my face sobered me up pretty damn fast. He was primal, animalistic in his attack.

He was fury driven, nothing more. Only when I was bleeding on the floor did he stop, and for the first time in our lives, he looked down on me. The hatred in his eyes staggered me. I'd always known that Nate felt he was second best, that he wanted everything I had. That included you, Addison. Even though our father treated him well, I was still his son, and Nate the mistake that broke our family apart. It was why Nate tried so hard, challenged me, made everything into a contest. He felt he had to win to become someone, never accepting himself for who he was because everyone knew he was my Father's bastard son. He must have rejoiced when you married him, thinking he'd finally beaten me.

His fury that night came from knowing he hadn't won at all, once he delivered the child and saw that it was the spitting image of me. He knew the baby wasn't his, and he hated me with a vengeance, swearing that he would make me suffer. He made good on his promise. He took you away, Addie, and left me with nothing but the grief of losing you and our child."

Garrett

"Come, I'll make us a fresh brew, and I'll tell you what I know," I steered her toward the kitchen and pulled the stool out for her to sit. Topping up the water in the machine and flicking the switch, I dashed away to the bedroom to retrieve the now cold coffees and snagged the old dressing gown from the back of the door before returning to a now dry-eyed Addison. Depositing the cups to the bench, I turned and draped the old, worn material over her shoulders, and she wriggled her arms into the oversized garment.

"Thanks," she said, tying the belt.
I was sorry to see those curves hidden away, but now at least, I could concentrate.
As I shuffled around the kitchen, I recited the story I'd rehearsed so many times, living it over and over in my head. To finally get it out, to share it with Addison was like hauling up the anchor and finally being able to set sail, moving forward after being trapped in windless waters for far too long.
"Nate took a lifetime of angst out on me that night. My getting you pregnant was the final straw. He told me the little boy was the spitting image of the baby photos my father once had hanging on his bedroom wall, the child had my colouring, blonde fuzz on his tiny head, and the moment you held him, he knew the child wasn't his. Somehow against all odds, I'd won again. He pushed

every slight, every hurt, every loss he'd ever known into his fists, and I wore the lot. I had no idea he had it in him. If I hadn't been drunk when that first hit landed, I'd probably have fought back, but I figured he had every right to be pissed at me, and that first punch dropped me to the floor. I never expected the rain of blows that followed. It was an onslaught, and by the time he climbed off me, my face was nothing but a bloody pulp. Kemu found me on the floor and mopped up the blood, straightened my broken nose and cleaned up the splits in my lip and brow. I was almost comatose with grief, knowing the lost baby had indeed been mine. I couldn't come to the hospital to see you; I was barely conscious. Kemu told me the following morning that Nate had flown you across to the mainland. The operation you needed required a specialist surgeon and equipment we don't have here on the island. I didn't know for the longest time if you'd survived. I hid away for weeks waiting for the pain to subside, the bruising and swelling diminished, disappeared, but the unbearable ache of losing you and our baby never went away.

I watched as she sipped her coffee. What was she thinking? The green eyes hooded and red-rimmed gave nothing away.

Shaking her head, she lowered her mug to the table and, with a heartfelt sigh, said, "I'm sorry, Garrett. But you at least got your beating all in one dose, whereas Nate administered mine bit by bit during our married life. I felt guilty for such a long time. I tried to hate you when Nate implied the loss of our baby had been your fault, but slowly along with the blackened eyes, bruises, split lips and cutting words, I began to hate Nate instead.

Looking back now, I can see the angry child that lived inside of him, the lonely little boy who craved to be and to have everything his brother had. Nate would have thrived on being the best at something, anything. And when finally he stood victorious when we married, with my belly swollen with his child, he thought he'd won. And then to discover the truth." Her eyes left mine as she whispered, "I feel sorry for him, and it's too late to make amends now.

Perhaps that was his plan when he called me to his bedside. Maybe he was telling me he was sorry, sending me back here to you, so I could discover the truth and get closure?"

I shrugged, shook my head, "I guess we'll never know for sure. But he's gone now, and he can't hurt you, us, anymore. I will never forgive him for raising his hand to you. The beating I took was nothing; he probably deserved to lash out, but to lay the blame at your door, was wrong on so many levels. After all, you were the pawn in his game to get back at me, and you nearly died. How can you forgive either of us for what you've endured at our stupidity?"

"We've all lost so much," she replied, "the baby, our happiness and one another. We've wasted so much time, but Nate has managed to restore some of what was lost. He's managed to bring us back together, righting the wrongs, and I, for one, am happy to finally leave the past where it belongs and start anew if that's where you want to go with this."

Taking her in my arms, I held her close, inhaling the scent of her hair; she was my everything. Yes, I wanted this.

"Morning, oh, sorry," Kemu said as he walked in on us in the kitchen, smiling to himself as he saw Addison wrapped in my arms, "I didn't mean to interrupt…."

"Yeah, but you're going to anyway," I grinned as I released Addie from the bear hug I held her in and instead draped my arm over her shoulders, "have we got a new fledgling?" I asked, spotting the box he carried.

"No, sadly. I picked this up from the morning ferry; it has the return address of Mr Alexander's lawyer," he said, putting it on the table and sliding it across to us.

"Oh, I'd forgotten that was on its way. Thanks, Kemu. I appreciate you bringing it up. Can I offer you a coffee?"

Kemu shook his head, his smile faltering as he looked at Addison, noting the red-rimmed eyes. "You alright, Miss?" he asked, concern lacing his voice.

"Better than alright, Kemu. It seems memories can be quite freeing," she replied.

Kemu frowned at me, "you didn't tell her? The doctor said she had to remember on her own."

"No, she did all the hard work herself," I said, smiling down at Addie, "everything is out in the open now, no more talking in circles." My smile turned to a frown as I turned my attention to the box, wondering what mischief it held.

"Then no, I'll pass on the coffee and leave you two to put the past behind you finally," Kemu said, flicking his eyes at the box and nodding at us both; he walked out humming to himself.

"Shall we?" I asked.

"We shall," she answered, lacing her fingers through mine, and we moved towards the box to finally put the past behind us.

Addison

Reaching for the knife and holding it above the heavy cardboard, I had a fleeting image of Nate and wondered if this was how he felt that night, holding that sharp little scalpel in his hand, ready to slice through the outer packaging to discover death and sadness within. Closing my eyes, I slipped the blade through the tape and flipped open the lid; my breath caught in my throat as the knife clattered to the floor. Oh my god, precisely how Nate would have felt. Sucker punched! Garrett's sharp intake of breath beside me told me he felt the same. Inserted in a plastic wallet was a birth certificate atop the pile of documents.

Child
First/given names(s):   Rhett Nathanial
Surname/family name: Alexander
Sex: Male
Date of birth: 20 July 2018
Mother
First/given name(s):   Addison
Surname/family name: Alexander
Father
First/given name(s):   Garrett
Surname/family name: Alexander

"He named our baby!" I whispered, cradling the wallet in my hands.

"I, well, I suppose he had too. The baby was almost full-term when we lost him; legally, he had to be named." Garrett shook his head, squeezing his eyes shut as tears started to build behind them; no, he wouldn't let them fall; there had been enough tears shed already. Sucking in a deep breath, he spoke, "I can't believe Nate gave our son the name he knew I hated to be called and to use his own as a second name, seems my half-brother was a bit of a jokester, fucking with us from the beyond the grave."

My mind flew back to that white room, with the overpowering disinfectant smell, the shrivelled man on the bed with the oxygen mask on his face, his breathless tone, "He wasn't mine. Rhett isn't my..."

"Garrett," I whispered, "That's what Nate was trying to tell me in the hospital. He wasn't talking about you; he was telling me that my son wasn't his. What else is in the box?"

Garrett rifled through the documents, finally turning the box on end and dumping them on the kitchen table. Most of the paperwork was to do with the business, which Garrett was now the sole owner of, but a sealed envelope caught my eye, and I pointed it out, "What's that?" He lifted it from the stack and frowned at the writing on the front before holding it out to me.

"Mystery lady rises again; it's addressed to Sonya."

I rolled the thin envelope between my fingers. Who the hell is this woman? She seems to be cropping up an awful lot. I think it's about time to visit the elusive Sonya.

"You up for a drive, babe?" huh, weird, the word babe rolled off my tongue as easily as it had back when we were a couple, and then it clicked; we were a couple again.

Garrett's grin lit the room; he'd picked up on it, too, a simple word that made such a difference.

"Sure thing, sweetheart, but I think breakfast is needed first," he laughed as my stomach grumbled loudly.

An hour later, fed, watered, and dressed in some light linen pants and a T-shirt, I slipped on another pair of flats and grabbed a hat as we walked out the door, the envelope with the address to our destination, held tightly in my grasp.

I was second-guessing the decision to eat breakfast as the SUV bounced on the cobblestones jostling the food around in my stomach. Crikey, the nerves alone had made me want to heave.

As we pulled up outside the residence, Garrett stared in amazement. "Woah, this is Jimmy's old place! Word was he'd left it to some relative, but it didn't look like this when he lived in it; there's been some big money spent here." We glanced at one another, both wondering the same thing, was that big money, Nate's? It was easy to see where the builders had added an extension to the existing property, new cladding and paint job, with a stunning balcony set with outdoor furniture. As we climbed from the car, the sound of screaming kids came from down the garden. We caught sight of a couple of boys, possibly six or seven years old, running around the trees, shirts and shorts soaking wet, guns out and spraying jets of water toward the bushes where the screams were coming from. Happy kids, playing outside and having fun together, it was nice to see. But as good as the entertainment was, we were here for answers.

"Looks like fun," Garrett grinned as he laced his fingers through mine.

I gave him a strained smile, my nerves making me jittery. What would we unearth here? Did I really need to know if Nate had been cheating on me? Should I just walk away, close out that whole chapter of my life and move forward with Garrett? No! Sonya was part of that chapter; I needed to hear the entire story before closing this book.

Opening the gate, we entered the property, making sure to close it again behind us and headed for the front of the house. Garrett's grip on my hand tightened as we mounted the steps, he seized the door-knocker and struck the door twice before releasing it, and we stood and waited.

A few moments later, a disembodied voice called out, "Who is it?"

Garrett and I looked at one another, and I nodded for him to answer.

"Yeah, um, hi, we're looking for Sonya Lawrence, my brother Nathanial Alexander sent us."

A key rattled in the lock, and then the door swung wide, revealing an olive-skinned, dark-haired woman with large brown eyes, her body shielded behind the open door, almost hiding as if she were frightened or nervous.

"I'm Sonya." She said softly, "Please come in. I've been expecting you." She extended her arm, an invitation showing which way for us to go.

Garrett let go of my hand and nudged me forward, his hand resting on the base of my spine, warming me, letting me know he was with me every step of this journey. I walked past the woman and down the hallway entering a bright, cheerful kitchen. Sonya closed the door and followed behind Garrett, passing us as we stood awkwardly inside the doorway.

"Please, sit." She indicated the chairs at the kitchen table. Garrett moved, pulled a chair out for me. I perched gingerly on the edge of the seat, uncomfortable, nervous, ready to sprint, make a break for it. I didn't want to be here!

"I'm Garrett, and this is...."

"I know who you are," she said quickly, "it's nice to meet you, Addison finally." Meet me; why would she have wanted to meet me? I inclined my head in acknowledgement of her greeting but kept silent, not knowing what to say.

"Have we met before; you seem very familiar?" Garrett said, and I looked at him in surprise before turning to study the woman once more.

"No," she replied quietly. "But you knew my dad, Jimmy, he owned this place, and when he died, he willed it to me."

"Oh, I didn't realize Jimmy had kids," Garrett responded, surprise evident in his voice.

"And of course, you may remember my mother from ..." She was cut short as the back door banged open and the two young boys we'd seen in the garden earlier stood dripping in the doorway.

"Mum, we need some towels, and can we have ice cream?" they asked and then noticed there were visitors in the room. They both glanced at Garrett, who was still standing up and then dropped their eyes to me where I still perched on the edge of the seat and stared, wide-eyed.

"Mum, is that?"

"Yes," she barked, effectively shutting them down. "Back outside now boys, I'll bring towels and ice cream out shortly."

I stared at them, dark hair, olive skin. Both a pint-sized replica of Nate and my stomach heaved. It seemed I had my answer. But how old were they? How long had the affair been going on? Oh god. I was going to be sick.

"Toilet," I whispered, "please, I need to use the toilet." My breathing was heavy, almost panting as I tried to retain my breakfast.

"Second on the left," Sonya said, pointing at the door to the hall. I got up and ran. Reaching for the bathroom door, I launched myself to my knees and vomited violently into the bowl. Wiping my mouth on some toilet paper, I flushed the loo but couldn't find the strength in my shaking limbs to move. So, I sat, leaning against the wall and wishing the floor would open up and swallow me whole. I glanced through the door I'd left open in my haste and sat up straight as I saw a wall of photographs in the bedroom opposite. Dragging myself to my knees, I crawled forward and, checking that Sonya nor Garrett could see, slunk across the hallway and through the open doorway and stared.

"How old are your boys?" I heard Garrett asking.

"TJ and James are almost seven, and then there's Jake, who's four," she answered. "They're good kids, considering the upheaval of losing their father; he died in a motor accident, and then their grandad passed away, and now Nate. They are a wonder, so resilient."

What, so they aren't Nates boys? But they look so much like him!

"You were saying I might know your mother?" Garrett reminded her gently.

Yes, Garrett, keep her talking, find out what you can.

"Oh, and Nate left this for you." I heard the rustle of paper as he handed her the envelope I'd left on the table.

"Thank you, um yes, Coral Harper, you would have only been a child when she left the island, though." I heard the tear of paper as she ripped open the envelope, and then there was silence. What was going on? I couldn't hide in here any longer. I stood and walked back toward the kitchen with shaking legs, leaving the room which housed a shrine to me. Was that where Nate slept when he would visit? Had he wallpapered it with photographs of me? Things were getting more and more confusing.

"Nate was your half-brother," Garrett couldn't keep the shock from his voice as he stared at the woman across the room.

"Um, I thought Nate would have told you. Yes, his mother is my mother. When she left here all those years ago, Jimmy went with her, they were together for a couple of years, but sadly Jimmy was an island person, he wasn't happy in the city. They broke up. Mum didn't tell him about me until I was in my teens, and my boys and I were lucky enough to get to know him before he died. When I discovered he left me the house, I decided to move here, and mum finally told me about Nate. I didn't meet him until TJ broke his arm, and I took him to the hospital. But after that, Nate visited often, we were close, and he came to stay when he could."

"But why did he never mention you?" I ask, unbelieving that I'd had a sister-in-law that I'd never know existed.

"I don't know. Nate was an angry person. I know he mistreated you, Addison, but he kept assuring me that one day you'd retrieve your memories and then you'd visit."

Shaking my head as if that would help clear this confusion, this made no sense whatsoever. Why hadn't he told me about her? Why keep her such a secret? Hell, even his lawyer didn't know their relationship. What did my memory loss have to do with any of this? So many questions.

"Nate's lawyer seemed to think you could answer any questions we may have. But I honestly don't know what needs answering now unless to let me know you are related to him. But with the divorce, that doesn't seem likely."

Sonya frowned, "What? You don't know why Nate sent you here?" The confusion in her voice rivalled my feelings exactly.

"Um, maybe there's something in the letter from the lawyer. Would you care for a drink while I have a quick read?"

"A glass of water would be lovely," I answered, anything to wash away the lingering acidic bite from being sick.

Garrett pulled a chair closer to mine, and we sat together on one side of the table as Sonya deposited the glasses in front of us and, with a timid smile, sat opposite us, withdrew the letter from its envelope and smoothed out the folds. Garrett and I sat silent, the heat of his hip touching mine, helping to keep me calm as I sipped the cool refreshing water as I peered over the edge of my glass at Sonya's ever-changing expressions as she read.

A tear glistened, then fell, then another and another as I watched with growing discomfort. Maybe this was something Sonya should have read in private. Her face paled, her watery eyes lifted, locked onto mine, and I saw disbelief, sadness, anger and fear in her face.

"No, no, no, Nate. You didn't." Her tears fall unchecked as she reached for my hand. "I am so, so sorry, Addison. I didn't know. He loved you so much." She shook her head and pulled her hand back, picking up the envelope and pulled a photograph from within; she studied it for a long moment before putting it face-down on the table.

What the hell was happening? What had Nate done to cause this reaction?

Sonya took a deep breath and let it out slowly, regaining control.

"Nate had a funny way of showing love," I ground out. "He beat me black and blue for two years."

"He was an angry man. He'd been cheated on, lied to, he lost what he wanted most in his life, a family of his own." Her face changed, anger bleeding through, "You hurt him, both of you destroyed him, and because of that, he wanted to destroy you too. What he did would have done just that, but his plan backfired because you lost your memories, Addison. You didn't remember the night your son was born, the night you broke Nate's heart."

Tears gathered in my eyes. "I remembered this morning, Sonya. I'm so sorry that we hurt Nate. It wasn't intentional; the whole story was one fucked up mess, starting in a bottle of tequila."

"So that's the reason you're here. You know about Rhett...."

"Yes," Garrett cut in. "She knows he was my son, not Nates. But he's gone! It's time to move forward." Sonya ignored him, keeping her gaze on me.

"Nate would have been a spectacular father, Addison. He spent so much time here with his nephews; he loved them, spoiled them rotten. Nate did this place up; said it was for me, but I knew it was more for the boys. He plastered your face over a wall in the bedroom; he always kept you close, part of the family. My brother never got over the loss of wanting to be a dad; Nate wanted more than anything to have a child with you, and when you didn't fall pregnant, blamed you, even though he suspected and the tests proved it, it was him! Nate couldn't give you a baby, and so he let you go. My brother came and stayed here for weeks after you left him, and he confessed that he'd hit you, hurt and lied to you. The grief and guilt weighed heavily. I didn't realize what he felt so guilty about; yes, he was wrong to hit you. I didn't understand the full story until now." Her eyes moved to the letter.

"Spit it out, Sonya," Garrett growled from beside me. "What was in the letter?"

"An explanation. A confession, and this!" She answered, turning the photograph over.

Like a black and white television show, the colour faded from our faces, from the room as both Garrett and I studied the image before us. "How?" I whispered. I was staring at my blood-covered self, cradling a newborn baby.

The backdoor flew open, slamming into the bench with a loud bang. Startled, we watched four little boys battle their way through the entrance and run into the kitchen. The three with dark hair skidded to a halt when they saw us watching, but the fourth, the odd one out with his overly long blonde hair, kept coming. He shrieked as he ran. "Momma, Momma," he launched himself onto my lap, his little arms wrapping around my neck as his wet clothes seeped into mine. My arms raised and clutched this wee fellow tightly. "Momma," he whispered in my ear. "You're all better now? Uncle Nate said you would come when you were better."

Garrett

Watching in disbelief as a mini-me ran across the room directly to Addison. He called her Momma, and there was no mistaking who this little boy was, but how? We lost him!

Reluctantly, I tore my shocked gaze from the most beautiful image ever, the love of my life rocking back and forth holding my son, her arms wrapped around him and his around her, and looked to Sonya's now pale face for answers.

Sonya shook her head, her eyes darting back and forth between Addison and myself, then leant forward, pushing Nate's letter across the table and nodding for me to read for myself the confession our half-brother had written.

Dear Sonya

Thank you. Thank you. Thank you. I can never say that enough for all you have done for Rhett and me. I don't deserve you and your kindness, and you certainly don't deserve what I'm going to ask of you now.

I'm so sorry! If you are reading this, then this cancer has seen me off. I've covered you and your boys financially; please never worry about that. You are a fantastic person! Thank you for looking after Rhett for me while we waited for Addison to regain her memories; quite possibly, she's done that by returning to the island and seeing Garrett again and may even be with you as you read this.

You know the story of the night Rhett came into this world, that Addison's accident caused his early arrival. I refrained from mentioning that Addison woke up, she was lucid whilst we worked on her to save the child's life and stem the bleeding. She spoke, called for Garrett and as the nurse lay our baby on Addison's chest, she cried and called him 'baby Rhett'. To say I was shocked is an understatement, but as I studied the child, I realized she was stating the truth, not naming the child. Addison suddenly began to seize, and I forgot about the baby until we had her stabilized once more, but she never regained consciousness. I decided to fly her to the city, and I brought her son to you for safekeeping.

There was so much going on! Addison unconscious, the early birth of the baby, shock, disbelief and anger. So much anger, Sonya. All my life, I'd played second fiddle to my half-brother, and to discover he had cheated me, taken my wife, my family and what should have been my future was too much. I'm not proud of my actions, but that night I needed payback. I went home to collect a bag, and Garrett was there. I saw red, and I beat him to a pulp leaving him to bleed physically and emotionally as I left him believing that the child had died. I wanted to hurt him, and I knew it would only be days before he found out the truth once Addison regained consciousness. I couldn't have foreseen that Addison would lose her memory, and yet it was a delicious thought that Garrett would be writhing in pain thinking he'd caused the death of his child. I waited and then waited some more. But Addison never remembered that she'd held Rhett. As days passed, I found it more and more difficult, never finding the right time to come clean about the child or confront her on the charge of infidelity; but Addison could read the anger and grief on my face and concluded that she'd lost the child. Her guilt and pain were palpable. I felt vindicated; this was an act of revenge I could work to my benefit.

I never felt guilty for lying to her; after all, she'd lied to me, tit for tat. I planted the seeds of doubt, watered and nurtured the suggestion that Garrett had caused her accident.

All I wanted was a family! And when I discovered I couldn't father a child, I was merciless. Addison wore the brunt of my angst. I pushed the blame on her, and she left me, knowing she couldn't give me what I craved when the truth was the exact opposite.

I lied to her, I lied to Garrett, and I lied to myself. But my dear, dear sister, I am so sorry because I lied to you too and now you have to right all my wrongdoings.

I asked you to keep Rhett for me, hidden away awaiting Addison's restored health. I told you that she wasn't strong enough, needed more time. And that she would come for him as soon as she was better. And I said to you that Garrett never wanted the child. Each visit, I gave Rhett assurance that his Momma would come for him when she was better. I love my nephew, but I've betrayed him as well. I let him believe Addison would be coming for him when in reality, she didn't know he existed. I never told her, as I led you to think I had. How could I, Sonya? How could I tell a grieving mother that her son was alive and healthy, knowing the truth would have cost me my wife?

I am sorry, Sonya. Please forgive me, and I pray one day, Addison and Garrett will forgive me too. Look after yourself and my three nephews.

Your loving brother
Nate.

With tears in my eyes, I looked from the letter to Addison, her face still bewildered as our son grabbed her hand, "come and see my room, Momma, you are on my wall," he stated, pulling her from her seat and dragging her down the hallway.

"Wait," she whispered and stopped the little boy. "Can your daddy come too?" She held her hand out to me. Rhett looked at me then, watched as I took Addie's hand in mine and gave me a shy smile.

"Sure," he said, "Daddy can come too."

Epilogue

Three months later.

Screams erupted from Rhett as he opened the gate to discover his birthday present. The pony stood basking in the morning sunshine, tail swishing, saddled, ready and waiting for our son to take his first ride.
"A pony," he screeched. "I wanna ride her."
"Ride him," his aunty corrected him as she walked out of the house, followed by her boys. "Happy Birthday, Rhett," she sang out as she walked over to where I sat, watching as Garrett showed our son the correct way to greet Pedro, the pony, and gave me a big hug as she sat next to me. Rhett's cousins headed towards Garrett, standing in line and waiting their turn for a pony ride.
I never tire of the sight of my two favourite men, one a doppelganger of a much younger Garrett.
They'd gotten so close since that momentous day at Sonya's home. Garrett loved his son, spending time showing him the eggs and baby chicks while telling him stories about growing up here with Rhett's Uncle Nate. The last three months had been a whirlwind.
We redecorated my old room for Rhett, blue walls with silver stencils of his favourite animals. We dumped my old bed and mirrored drawers in one of the spare rooms and replaced them with a sporty car bed that held pride of place surrounded by colourful cabinets and a small chair and table with boxes of crayons, pens and paper.

The main suite had also had a make-over. Nate's belongings cleared out, his medical journals donated to the hospital and Sonya taking what she wanted as a keepsake of her half-brother for herself and Nate's nephews. A total clean start, a brand-new chapter.

The sunlight glinted on my new wedding band, Garrett, and I finally tied the knot, making me Mrs Alexander for the second time and with my new best friend, Sonya standing beside me as my maid of honour.

"Have you told him yet?" Sonya whispered, bumping my shoulder gently.

Shaking my head, I smiled at her and pulled the image from the sonogram out of my pocket.

"What if it's all too soon. We've only just become parents to a four-year-old. What if he isn't ready to take on a baby too? You do realize this is all Nate's fault. If he hadn't lied to me, hadn't told me I couldn't conceive, then I would have been more careful, used protection," I sighed. "No, I haven't told him. I was waiting for you; I need back up just in case things don't go as I hope."

"He'll be thrilled, Addie," Sonya wrapped her arm around my shoulders, "and he isn't my hot-headed brother. Garrett would never lay a finger on you in anger. Tell him," she urged.

Nodding, I turned back to the boys as Rhett ran towards me. "Momma, did you see I rode Pedro? Did you watch?"

"Yes, baby, I was watching. Do you love your present?"

Rhett nodded emphatically. "Would you like to give Daddy a present?" I asked, and he nodded again. "Here," I handed him the photograph. "Go and give this to Daddy and say, 'Surprise Daddy!'"

Rhett took the photo and ran back down the path to the gate where Garrett was helping TJ into the saddle.

"Daddy, Daddy, I have a present for you from Momma," he said, waving the slip of paper around in the air.

Garrett grinned and ruffled his son's blonde hair, took the photograph from him, and stared hard at the grey and white picture; he raised his head to stare at me, and I nodded. He smiled and rounded the gate.

Rhett followed his father as he ran up the path and watched, giggling as I was picked bodily from my seat and swung round and round.

"Good surprise?" I asked a little breathlessly.

Garrett's lips found mine, and the searing heat filled kiss was answer enough.

Acknowledgments

I'd like to thank all my readers for taking the time to read my work.

Deborah Carter was born in the UK and moved to New Zealand as a child. She is a wife, mother of 5 and grandmother to 7. Works full time and spends free time reading and writing. Favourite book genre - vampires, shifters, romance.